POTION MASTERS

THE ETERNITY ELIXIR

FRANK L. COLE

SHADOW
MOUNTAIN

Library of Congress Cataloging-in-Publication Data

Names: Cole, Frank, 1977– author.

Title: The eternity elixir / Frank L. Cole.

Description: Salt Lake City, Utah : Shadow Mountain, [2017] | Series: Potion masters ; book 1 | Summary: "Aspiring Potion Master Gordy Stitser must prevent the Eternity Elixir from falling into the hands of the rebel Elixirists who are working to release the most powerful potion master of all time and take over the world"—Provided by publisher.

Identifiers: LCCN 2017012775 (print) | LCCN 2017026585 (ebook) | ISBN 9781629735597 | ISBN 9781629723587 (hardbound : alk. paper)

Subjects: | CYAC: Magic—Fiction. | Magicians—Fiction. | LCGFT: Fantasy fiction. | Novels.

Classification: LCC PZ7.C673435 (ebook) | LCC PZ7.C673435 Et 2017 (print) | DDC [Fic]—dc23

LC record available at https://lccn.loc.gov/2017012775

Printed in the United States of America

Lake Book Manufacturing, Inc., Melrose Park, IL

10 9 8 7 6 5 4 3 2 1

For Heidi, Jackson, Gavin, and Camberlyn.
Your stories are the reason why I write.

1

The creature, all bristly hair and quivering bulbs of pus, slithered in from the kitchen, dragging its enormous knuckles along the floor. Slime trailed behind it as it entered the living room to where Isaac and Jessica Stitser, eight-year-old twins, sat in front of the television, watching Saturday morning cartoons and balancing bowls of Cinnamon Burst cereal in their laps.

Jessica glanced up from her cereal and gawked at the creature before releasing a fit of giggles.

"Move over," the creature growled.

The twins slid over to make room, and the slime-covered monstrosity released a depressing sigh before plopping down between them on the couch.

"Gordy, what are you doing?" Mrs. Stitser said as she hurried down the stairs. "You're ruining the upholstery!"

"It didn't work," the creature groaned, a stream of drool dropping from its lower lip.

Mrs. Stitser folded her arms and scowled. "I can see that. You're a mess!"

The creature scratched the edge of a boil on its forehead and whimpered. "I'm getting slobber all over my favorite shirt." A putrid stain had already begun forming across the numbers of its Cleveland Browns jersey.

"We can't hear the show!" Isaac shouted.

"Come on, guys. Can't you see I'm having an emergency here?" the creature said, but then lowered its voice. "Why didn't it work?"

"How should I know?" Mrs. Stitser asked.

"Mom!" the creature howled.

"Gordy!" She stifled a laugh.

"Be quiet!" Jessica smacked one of the couch cushions angrily.

Mrs. Stitser rolled her eyes as she bent down and turned off the television, which caused an immediate eruption from the twins.

"We weren't finished with our show!" Isaac yelled.

"Go upstairs and get dressed," she said. "You can watch cartoons later."

Though they whined, the twins obeyed and stomped up the stairs.

"You didn't follow the directions like I told you, did you?" she asked Gordy once his younger siblings had left.

Gordy bobbed his head and held up a misshapen blob in protest. "I did. Catfish eyes, a handful of silver flakes, four pieces of birch bark, a mill worm cut in half—"

"Which cauldron did you use?"

"The copper one," Gordy answered immediately.

"And how much ginger wax?"

"Six ounces. I filled up the blue measuring cup like you told me. Not an ounce more. I even weighed it on the electronic scale."

Gordy's mom frowned. "And you lit the Amber Wick?"

"Uh-huh. And blew it out after three seconds."

"Did you use the stopwatch or did you try to Mississippi it? It has to be exactly three seconds."

"I did it right!"

She folded her arms and sat down on the edge of the love seat. Closing her eyes, she quietly mumbled the list of instructions for Gordy's potion. Then she asked, "Which feather did you use?"

Gordy scrunched his bulbous brow. "Feather? There was no feather." His voice grew agitated as his mom smirked. Fishing a folded piece of paper containing the potion instructions out of a slimy fold of his body, Gordy furiously scanned the page and gripped the edges tightly. "A blue jay feather? How did I miss that?"

His mom shook her head. "You'll have to start from scratch."

Gordy's eyes widened. "Start all over? I don't want to waste the rest of my Saturday."

"You're the one who wants to make the perfect costume for the school Halloween party. A potion like that takes time."

"Fine," Gordy huffed, staring down at his beefy, boil-riddled arms. "I'll just use what I have. I look better as a bloated monster anyways."

"You can't show up for school looking like that. Your costume has to be discreet. Seamless," his mom said. "Otherwise they'll put pictures of you in the newspaper. Rule number one, Gordy. Never draw unnecessary attention to the potion community."

The boil on Gordy's forehead popped and purple ooze dripped from the hole. "How long am I going to look like this?"

"Three seconds of the Amber Wick equals three hours of normal time. And you're going to clean my couch before I leave for the convention, you know that, right?"

Gordy stood and looked down at the dark, damp spot where he had been sitting. "When do you leave?" he asked, covering the stain with a floral pillow.

"Tomorrow morning. Early. I'll need you to wake up with me so I can run through the list before I go."

"How early?" Gordy narrowed one bloodshot eye.

"Five o'clock. Don't give me that look," she scolded.

Gordy flinched in surprise, wondering how exactly his mother had picked up on his annoyed expression despite his current state of blobbiness.

"Until your father comes home tomorrow evening, you're the man of the house and that means you take on extra responsibility," she said. "Autumn is always a strenuous season for his line of work."

Gordy's dad sold a wide variety of appliances all over the country. He specialized in dishwashers, but he knew just about everything there was to know about anything you could find in a kitchen. Mr. Stitser didn't share his wife's or his son's talent for potion-making, but he had always been extremely supportive.

And though Gordy may have forgotten one crucial ingredient to his costume potion, when compared to other Drams of his age, he towered above all in natural skill. As an adolescent brewer of potions, Gordy still had a few years to go before he graduated from a Dram to a full-scale Elixirist, but he was well on his way. Wanda Stitser, Gordy's mom, fully appreciated her son's talent. An Elixirist, fourth-class, Wanda was one of the greatest concocters of potions in the country.

As they entered the kitchen, Gordy's mom grabbed the roll of paper towels from the counter and handed her son several sheets.

Grumbling, Gordy dropped the towels on the floor and with one bloated foot, wiped the slime from the linoleum.

Chicxulub Asteroid Crater, Chicxulub, Mexico

Mounds of dirt, rock, and clay ringed a massive hole where two dozen sweat-soaked men jabbed their shovels into the earth. Only the tops of the workers' hats and bandanas could be seen in the glaring headlights of a white SUV. It was just after two o'clock in the morning, and the digging had been underway for several hours.

A woman with spiky blonde hair and bright red lipstick sat rigid in the driver's seat of the idling vehicle, watching the ongoing excavation. Occasionally, she would reach over and brush her hand across a weathered, leather satchel resting in the seat next to her.

"Have they finished yet?" a man with a heavy Russian accent asked from the back of the SUV. "I'm almost out of battery, and I didn't bring my phone charger." He lay sprawled across the backseat, playing a game on his cell phone.

"That's not my problem," the woman said.

"No, it's not, but it's going to get awfully boring in here soon." The man was in his mid-forties and had light-gray hair and a thick barrel chest that provided the perfect prop for his electronic device. "If I don't have something to occupy my time, I'm going to start talking to you again. And we both know how much you hate that."

"I don't hate talking with you"—she glanced down at her manicured nails—"when you have something intelligent to offer." Unlike her companion, the woman spoke with an elegant British accent, her words pouring from her lips with the consistency of melted chocolate.

"Is that an invitation to sit up front then?" The man placed his hands on the tops of the seats and began to hoist himself over the center console.

"Wait!" Her hand shot up.

Dust no longer rose from the hole. The digging had stopped. The two occupants of the vehicle watched as one of the workers clambered out, waving his hands in the air.

"*¡Hemos encontrado algo!*" the man shouted.

The woman pressed the button on her armrest, and the window lowered an inch. "In English, *por favor!*" she snapped.

"We found something, *señora!* *Una caja* . . . er, I mean a box."

The smell of dirt and sweat filled the woman's nostrils as she exited the SUV and approached the excavation. The worker who had delivered the news jabbed his shovel into the center of the hole, and the hollow tin of metal sounded.

As the man lifted the box, the woman eyed the padlock securing the container before reaching out and seizing it from the man's hands.

"This is it!" she declared.

"That is it?" her Russian companion asked, his brow furrowing. "Seems pretty teeny to be capable of taking down B.R.E.W."

"Hush!" the woman snapped. "Hand me my bag. Quickly! I need to check it for Dire Substances." As she turned and reached out her hand to her Russian companion, one of the workers, a boy in his mid-teens, suddenly burst through the crowd of onlookers. The woman yelped in surprise as the boy yanked the box from her grip and bolted away with incredible speed.

"Grab him!" she shouted.

But none of the workers had a chance to lay a finger on the boy before he was past the SUV and racing into the dark.

The Russian took out his gun and fired.

The young thief dodged left and right, the bullets whizzing harmlessly past him in the air.

"I'm not that bad of a shot," the Russian said. By the time he had reloaded his weapon, the boy had vanished from sight.

"Save your bullets," the woman said, a thin smile forming on her lips. "That young man has been Blotched. Even if you were to strike him, he'd keep running until he delivered the package or bled out. Impressive work."

"Who do you think did this?" the Russian asked.

"It's obvious, isn't it?" The woman slid back into the driver's seat of the SUV. "He was under *her* control."

The man scratched his head. "I thought you took measures to keep her in the dark."

"She's more powerful than I gave her credit."

"What about them?" The man looked at the workers leaning upon their shovels, muttering to each other in Spanish.

"What *about* them?" she asked.

"We could have a problem. These men are expecting payment."

"Then pay them and be done with it." She slammed the door and turned the key in the ignition. The engine roared to life.

The man chuckled. "Me? Pay them? I don't have any money."

"Well, then." She put the SUV into reverse. "That *is* a problem, isn't it?" The tires peeled out as she sped away, leaving the Russian behind, dodging the spray of dust and gravel.

A taxi idled in front of the Stitser home as Gordy
helped the driver load his mom's bags in the trunk.
The concrete driveway felt cool beneath Gordy's
bare feet, and he yawned before wiping the sleep from his
eyes. He stared up at the twinkling stars overhead; there
was absolutely no sign of the sun anywhere to be seen.

Gordy's mom had a flight in less than two hours to
Topeka, Kansas, where she would be the keynote speaker
at an important convention. She was always leaving early
in the morning or catching red-eye flights after midnight.
Gordy had grown accustomed to hefting his mother's suitcases into the trunks of taxis. For the moment, the Stitsers
owned only one working vehicle—the family van. The
other, a Subaru station wagon, remained lifeless in the garage. Gordy's mom had allowed a trusted colleague to pour
one of his special automotive concoctions into the gas tank,
rendering it inoperable—at least for another week or two.

On her way out the door, Gordy's mom ran through a

short list of particulars. "You've got my cell number memorized, and here's the information of the hotel where I'll be staying should you run into any sort of trouble. Of course you won't be able to reach me there until this evening, but I'll call you as soon as I land." She leaned forward and kissed Gordy on the cheek. "Also, try to spray Bawdry at least once with the room freshener before tomorrow. He's beginning to smell."

Gordy nodded. He had expected Bawdry to be on her list.

"And lastly, I want the twins staying up late tonight," she said.

Gordy started to nod his head once more, but caught himself mid-bobble. "You *want* them to stay up late?" That was an odd request. It was Sunday night. A school night.

"Isaac's coming down with a bit of a cold," she said, flipping one hand absently as she rummaged in her purse with the other. "I'd like to see where it takes him before I cure it. I have a new mucus-reducing potion I've created and I need test samples. So feed him plenty of sweets and have them watch something scary on the television." She patted her pockets. "Am I forgetting something?"

Gordy shrugged. "I don't think so." He nibbled on his thumbnail and nudged a rock with his toe. Now was the time to ask the question he had been pondering all weekend long.

"Mom?" Gordy's voice took on a softer, more

meaningful tone. "Before you go, is it all right that I asked Max and Adilene to come over later today?"

"Of course. Why would I care if they come—" His mom straightened abruptly and she fixed Gordy with a stern expression. "You mean come over to the lab?"

Gordy grinned and sucked back on his teeth, trying his best to look hopeful and deserving of having his wishes granted.

"I don't think so," she said. "The lab's in disarray. There are ingredients strewn about for projects that aren't to be tampered with, and Bawdry has reached near toxic levels—"

"We won't touch anything marked volatile," Gordy insisted. "I know which ingredients to avoid. And I'll spray Bawdry like you asked. Twice, even."

His mom sighed, her eyes softening just a smidge. Then they narrowed, and Gordy wasn't certain which way she would lean.

The cab driver cleared his throat and pointedly looked at his watch.

She turned and sighed. "Yes, yes, I'm coming." She swiveled back to Gordy and patted his shoulder. But before she could make her decision, which appeared to be leaning toward a firm "not this time," Gordy blurted out, "I'm almost twelve and a half, and I don't have any lab partners. You said that I needed some my own age. How am I supposed to become an Elixirist without lab partners?"

"Do you really want to get into an argument with me

over Max and Adilene?" She narrowed her eyes. "They're not even supposed to know about our secret."

What a disaster that had been! Gordy had invited his two best friends over for dinner without clearing it with his parents first. But how was he supposed to know that there had been a mishap with one of his mom's growth potions and that she had left the door open to air out the lab? Before he knew it, Max and Adilene had come face-to-face with a mill worm the size of a Rottweiler. So much screaming. Mostly from Max. After they calmed down, which took a few hours, his two friends had demanded answers, which Gordy felt he had to provide.

"But, Mom, they're smarter than you give them credit for, and they both volunteered!"

"Oh, I know they're smart, Gordy. They're your friends, and they're great kids. And of course they volunteered. Who wouldn't want to be a part of what we do? But you need *Dram* lab partners," she said. "Max and Adilene don't have the gift. They'll never be Elixirists."

"But they could learn, with my help," Gordy insisted. "And they haven't told a soul about our secret."

She smiled. "Didn't you have something to do with that?"

Gordy shrugged. His mom had wanted to wipe their memories completely, but Gordy had talked her into letting him give them a vial of Turkish Gizli Goop instead. It would prevent them from spilling the beans, and was a much safer procedure.

"There are several kids who would be perfect Dram lab partners," his mom said. "Dez Mumphrey lives just a half mile away."

"And he's allergic to everything, including the air," Gordy said. "One whiff of Bawdry and he'll explode!"

"When I get back, we'll sit down and discuss appropriate lab partners for you. Ones who can better assist your advancement."

Gordy opened his mouth to protest but struggled to find the words. It was too early in the morning and he felt fuzzy-headed from the smell of taxi exhaust. If only he had gone to bed at a reasonable hour instead of staying up well past midnight mixing potions in the lab. Then he would've been better prepared for this argument. Now what would he tell his friends? They had been so excited when they talked about their plans on their way home from school.

"They're my best friends, Mom," Gordy muttered. "And I trust them." He stared at his feet, his shoulders slumping in defeat as he awaited his mom's verdict.

She tapped her toe impatiently on the asphalt, and then groaned. "Oh, fine."

Gordy screwed up his face in confusion. "So . . . they can come over?" She didn't answer, but Gordy leaped in the air, punching his fist above his head.

"But believe me, bub, I have my vials logged. I know the exact amounts in every bottle and if I notice one cork has been slipped from anything kept in the bottom left-hand drawer, you'll be banished from the lab until further notice."

Gordy nodded vigorously. "Agreed. Absolutely! And we won't hang out long in the lab, I promise."

"No, you won't. An hour tops and then it's back upstairs with the twins. And no allowing Max to sneak a peek at Bawdry. Keep him zipped, clean up your mess, and lock the door when you're done. Understood?"

Gordy saluted, his cheeks crinkling from his widening smile. "Understood."

His mom grinned. "This is a big step for you. Lab partners." She stared past Gordy as if caught up in a memory. "I want a full report the moment I land. I'll be back by"—she fished her travel arrangements from her purse and checked her itinerary—"three o'clock tomorrow afternoon."

She gave Gordy one last kiss on the cheek for good measure and then she was gone.

Gordy bounded down the basement stairs, cycled through the combination lock, and then heaved open the heavy metal door to the Stitser lab. He instinctively ducked beneath a drying rack hooked to the ceiling where all manner of plants and herbs dangled like the whiskers of a gigantic walrus. Toadflax, garlic, barberry, and arrowroot, to name a few. Three apothecary tables lined one of the side walls with multiple drawers bearing labels such as *Monarch Wings*, *Porcupine Quills*, and *Shaved Ivory*. A long oak table stood in the middle of the room with a collection of flasks, crucibles, and Bunsen burners. Embedded in the far wall was a suet-stained fireplace that pumped smoke through a vented chimney in the bricks. And stacked neatly against the stove were several pots of varying shapes and metals. "Cauldrons" as Gordy's mother preferred to call them.

A beige sign hung from a hook above the stove, listing the Five Rules of Potion Making.

1. Never draw unnecessary attention to the potion community.
2. Never administer a potion to anyone without first testing it out on yourself.
3. Never cause permanent bodily harm or death with a potion.
4. Never concoct a potion using banned ingredients.
5. Never enter the Forbidden Zones.

Specialized air freshener in hand, Gordy unzipped the plastic shield surrounding Bawdry. Even though he was wearing a gas mask, Gordy retreated a step from the smell. Yellowish vapors rose from the opening, and he unleashed a heavy spray from the can, filling the bag.

"Bawdry, you need a bath!" Gordy zipped up the shield, turned on the oscillating fan next to one of the apothecary tables, and waited for the noxious levels in the air to dissipate before removing the gas mask.

Bawdry didn't respond.

Bawdry couldn't respond.

That was because Bawdry was the mummified remains of King Bawdry of Mesopotamia. Gordy's mom had won him at an auction during one of her conferences two years ago. Now all manner of tubes, sensors, and wires ran out of the mummy's body, supplying numerous flasks and vials with fluid. High-level potion-making material. Stuff Gordy didn't dare fiddle with since he had no doubt those were the types of chemicals capable of the disastrous results his mom frequently warned him about. Spraying the inside of the bag with air freshener and the occasional changing of a flask or two was all his mother would permit Gordy to do.

"Can we come down now?" Gordy's best friend, Max Pinkerman, shouted from the top of the stairs.

Gordy glanced at a flowerpot resting next to King Bawdry's bag. A pale yellow flower was beginning to nudge its way out from its glistening green pod. "The canary bell-flower is blooming," he announced. "All clear."

The sound of charging footsteps filled the stairwell as Max bounded down to the basement level. Joining Gordy, Max stared at the mummy encased in its protective shielding. Max took in a deep breath and promptly gagged.

"Bleck! It still stinks in here."

Adilene descended the stairs with her fingers pinching her nostrils closed. "I hope it's safe," she said, her voice echoing. "Because if I end up poisoned or hexed in some way, I'm going to be very upset." Adilene was wearing her earbuds and the sound of heavy music thrashed out from under her long black hair.

"You won't get poisoned," Gordy assured her.

"What?" she shouted before removing one of the buds.

Gordy grinned. "What are you listening to?"

Adilene lived in the house kitty-corner to the Stitsers, and Gordy had been friends with her since her family moved to the neighborhood from El Salvador six years ago. She usually listened to much softer music.

Adilene frowned and glanced at her iPod. "This is uh . . . Cattle Slayer, I think."

"Why are you listening to that?" Max asked, scowling.

"It's for my end-of-term science project," Adilene said. "We have two weeks left before it's due, and I'm guessing you haven't even started. Have you, Maxwell?"

Max scoffed and swatted his hand dismissively. "I've got plenty of time. Besides, how does listening to that garbage have anything to do with science?"

Adilene smiled. "I'm studying the effects different music has on moods. Right now it's Death Metal, and I think it's making me angry."

Max snickered. "I don't think that's the music's fault." He gazed longingly at the murky bag where Bawdry slumbered and elbowed Gordy in the side. "What's it like?" The shield's material was too opaque to see through, though Gordy noticed Max trying, his eyes narrowing to slits so thin, they could've been sealed shut.

"He's gross," Gordy said. "Kind of like a meaty skeleton, but one that's wearing a cloth diaper." The mummy had been dead for centuries, but Gordy often felt sorry for the emaciated man, forced to reside in his plastic enclosure, wearing only his underwear. *Poor Bawdry*, Gordy thought.

"*¡Increíble!*" Adilene exclaimed, finally taking her eyes off Bawdry and absorbing the scenery of the Stitser lab. She plucked the remaining bud from her ear and silenced the clattering noise of Cattle Slayer. "This is it, no? Your mother's lab." She approached the closest apothecary table and timidly reached for one of the containers resting on the counter before withdrawing her hand. "May I?" she asked Gordy politely.

"Yeah, sure. Everything on that table is relatively safe," Gordy said. "Just be careful and don't spill anything."

Adilene carefully plucked one of the vials from the counter and read the label. She made a sour face. "Is this really koala kidneys?"

Gordy smiled. "If that's what it says."

Max grunted. "It's not from an actual koala. Probably just a fake one."

Adilene rolled her eyes. "Fake koalas?"

"You know what I mean," Max said.

Gordy took his two friends on a tour of the lab. Adilene asked a plethora of questions regarding the various containers of mysterious ingredients and their uses and functions. There were hundreds of vials, each carefully marked in Mrs. Stitser's near-perfect penmanship.

Max seemed interested, but he split his time listening to Gordy while keeping his eyes glued to Bawdry slumped in the corner. It was only Gordy pointing out the bottom left-hand drawer of the third apothecary table—the one Mrs. Stitser had strictly forbidden—that piqued Max's interest.

"What sort of stuff?" Max squatted to take a closer look at the drawer marked *Volatile*.

"Seriously, Maxwell, don't touch that!" Adilene had moved away from the table, her arms folded, her body tense and rigid.

"Chill out. I'm not touching anything," Max said, trying unsuccessfully to tug the drawer open.

"Sorry, guys. We can't even look in there." Gordy had never been allowed to even peek inside, but he figured it contained the most dangerous items of everything in the lab. He was positive his mom had some sort of alarm that would trigger at any intrusions.

"Well, this is all really cool," Adilene said. "It's just like you told us."

"Thanks." Gordy felt a sense of pride swelling in his chest.

For the past several years, ever since his mom first allowed him access to the basement, Gordy had been forced to keep the existence of the Stitser lab a secret. It was dangerous to let outsiders know about the potion community. At the time, Gordy hadn't understood why it was so dangerous, but he obeyed his mother's wishes just the same. His brother and sister vaguely understood that something was going on in the lab, but their mom had fed them a long-lasting potion of forgetfulness to prevent them from accidentally revealing the secret to one of their school friends. She had administered the same potion to Gordy when he had been the twins' age, but after a few days, the effects of the draught had mysteriously worn off. It had baffled his mom at first, until Gordy revealed to her how he had devised a concoction of his own which countered the forgetful nature of his mom's potion. His mom had taken him downstairs to the lab the very next day.

And now, here he was, showing Max and Adilene his secret world. The world of potion-making.

Max plucked a small vial of liquid from the counter and held it close to his eyes. "I can't even read this," he said. He reached out to set the vial back on the counter, but missed and nearly dropped it.

Luckily, the glass didn't shatter, but the vial rolled along the countertop, heading for the edge. Gordy was about to leap over to keep it from falling, but Adilene got there first.

"*¡Eres tan torpe!*" Adilene snapped, carefully catching the vial and handing it to Gordy. "Maybe we're not ready to be down here."

Gordy shrugged. Adilene was probably right. Neither one possessed the necessary skills to become an Elixirist. According to his mom, that was something you were born with. But Gordy didn't mind. Max and Adilene were his best friends, and as far as he was concerned, they made the perfect lab partners.

5

The delicious aroma of Chicken Cacciatore wafted through the kitchen as Gordy's mother removed the casserole dish from the oven. It was Monday evening, and Mrs. Stitser had returned home from her most recent trip, early for once. The Stitser family gathered around the dining room table, staring at a Mason jar.

Normally, Mrs. Stitser decorated with flowers or fruit or scented candles, but not tonight. This Mason jar had been sealed with a brass ring and contained a human tongue.

Saliva moistened the glass as the tongue flicked and rolled. Each time it performed a trick, one of the twins burst into laughter.

"Make it whistle!" Isaac reached across the table for the jar.

Gordy promptly slapped his hand away. "He can't make it whistle."

"Why not?" Jessica asked.

Gordy stared at his father sitting at the head of the table with his lips pursed tightly together. "Because it has to be in his mouth to do that."

Gordy's dad forced a smile. "En ehackly ill ee ee un?" he asked, which made absolutely no sense at all to Gordy. The twins snickered, but Gordy felt bad for his dad. He looked so uncomfortable.

"I'm so sorry, dear," Gordy's mom announced from the kitchen. "It'll be over soon. Just five more minutes, I promise. You're being such a good sport."

His dad rolled his eyes. "Ood ort!"

Gordy's dad had agreed to allow Mrs. Stitser to try out a new potion on him. It was supposed to render him completely silent, but as the Stitsers soon discovered, simply not having a tongue in one's mouth did not make one quiet.

Wanda Stitser carried in a piping hot casserole dish with her black oven mitts. A pleasant smell followed her into the room.

"Careful. It's really hot." Instead of placing the dish on the hot pad at the center of the table, she lowered it in front of Gordy and wafted the steam towards his nostrils. "Decipher," she instructed.

Gordy nodded and inhaled the aroma of tomatoes, poultry, and bow-tie pasta. He caught hints of oregano and garlic, but also something foreign. "Is that bloodroot?" he asked.

His mother beamed. "Yes. What else?"

Gordy knew bloodroot could be used to make someone

throw up, but why would his mom want that to happen at the dinner table?

Isaac drummed his fingers on the table impatiently. "Can we eat now?"

Mrs. Stitser ignored Isaac and smiled at Gordy, showing all her teeth, hinting at the answer.

Jessica's hand shot into the air. "Ooh, ooh! I know! You put teeth in it!"

"Teeth?" Isaac whined. "Why do we have to eat teeth?"

"It's not teeth, dear," Mrs. Stitser said. Though it wouldn't have been the first time a molar had snuck its way into a meal.

Gordy snapped his fingers. "Seal bone powder."

"Well done!" she cheered, finally setting the dish on the table.

"What's bone powder have to do with teeth?" Jessica asked.

"A potion made of bloodroot and the bones from an arctic seal makes you want to brush your teeth. Potion Master dentists used it all the time a hundred years ago," Gordy said.

"And it still works." His mom ladled servings of the meal onto everyone's plate. "I'm very proud of you, Gordy. I've said this many times before, but I have never seen anyone with your natural talent at Deciphering. It takes most Elixirists years to master the skill, and yet you're so young and so good."

Gordy ducked his head, embarrassed by the praise.

Isaac and Jessica rolled their eyes at each other. The twins perhaps had a future in potion making, but for the time being, they were far too impatient and stubborn to practice.

Eyeing his meal eagerly but without a tongue to assist in swallowing, Gordy's dad held up his hands in frustration.

"Oh, I'm so sorry, Gordon!" Mrs. Stitser pulled a small spray bottle from her apron pocket and lightly spritzed her husband's mouth. The tongue disappeared from the jar with a flashing pop.

"Finally!" Gordy's dad worked his tongue around in his mouth. "Remind me never to agree to that again."

"Come now," Wanda said, reaching over and caressing her husband's cheek. "Where would I be without my hero? Now, what's on everyone's schedules this week?" She pulled out her smartphone.

"I have a sales meeting on Thursday evening," Gordy's dad announced.

Wanda clucked her tongue. "I'm leaving Thursday for a convention, and I have to be at the airport no later than four o'clock."

Mr. Stitser slurped his drink. "That's a problem. My meeting with the Western Garbage Disposal Union starts at four thirty."

"That's nowhere near the airport." She narrowed her eyes and quickly thumbed a message in her online calendar. "Fine. I'll take a taxi . . . again."

"No, no, I'll drop you off," Mr. Stitser said, his mouth crammed with pasta and sauce. "I can be a little late. It's only garbage disposals."

Mrs. Stitser sighed and smiled. "Thank you, dear. It will be nice to save a bit of money. Taxi fares are bleeding our savings dry."

"But I do want my Subaru back sometime this year. How long is this *procedure*"—Mr. Stitser made air quotes—"going to take?"

"Just one more week, and life will be back to normal," she insisted.

"So Thursday looks to be jam-packed," Gordy's dad said. "What with my meeting and your convention, and, of course, that thing you're planning on taking Gordy to Thursday morning."

Gordy had been absently absorbing the mundane conversation of weekly schedules while scarfing down his dinner, but his ears perked up at his dad's mention of his name.

"What thing?" he asked, his eyes flitting between his parents.

His dad winked at Gordy.

His mom puckered her lips and scrunched her nose. "Always trying to spoil the fun, aren't you, buster?" she said to her husband. Wanda exhaled and shifted her gaze to Gordy. "I read in your curriculum that you could earn a significant amount of extra credit from spending some time at one of your parents' workplaces."

Gordy swallowed a bite, trying not to get his hopes up.

"I've cleared it with your principal. You'll spend half a day on Thursday with me, but you'll have some make-up work to do on Friday," she said. "So nothing but studying after school. You understand?"

"Are you serious?" Gordy scooted back from the table, the chair legs chirping as they scuffed against the wooden floor. "You're taking me to B.R.E.W. Headquarters?"

His mom dabbed at the corners of her mouth with a napkin before resting her hands on the table and offering Gordy the slightest of nods.

Gordy leaped from his chair, hooting and hollering in delight. His mom giggled. The twins watched from their seats, their faces contorted with confusion.

"Now, hold up," Mr. Stitser announced, raising a finger and cutting through Gordy's raucous celebration. "Gordy could very well choose to accompany me to work, Wanda. We can't just assume he's all that interested in visiting your mysterious headquarters. He needs to make his choice."

Gordy stopped abruptly. "Oh, yeah," he said, lowering into his chair. "I mean, of course I want to see where you work, Dad. I just . . ." He couldn't imagine having to listen to his dad yammer on and on about appliances all day long, but he didn't want to hurt his dad's feelings.

"Stop." Mr. Stitser swatted his hand, snickering. "I'm only kidding. Your mother's work is way more interesting than mine. Wouldn't want you to miss out on that opportunity."

Gordy smiled. "Thanks, Dad."

"Why don't we get to go?" Isaac asked. His lips were bright red from tomato sauce, and no doubt speckled with traces of bloodroot.

"Yeah," Jessica chimed in. "I want to have a day off from school."

"And you will, when you're old enough," Gordy's mom said. "But this is Gordy's time, and I think he's finally earned a chance to see where the real magic takes place."

6

ordy's mom navigated the van to the first of two security checkpoints and showed her badge to the uniformed man standing guard. The other guard gave Gordy a temporary pass which allowed him access to certain areas of the property. Gordy clipped the pass to his shirt and leaned forward to stare out through the windshield at the immense hexagonal-shaped building rising four stories above the expansive grounds.

At the second checkpoint, Gordy saw a bright pink sign with the words SOMNIUM FINE CREAMS AND OILS stuck in the lawn in front of a neatly manicured hedgerow. Bottles and cartons of various Somnium products were sold all over the country at grocery stores and in gas stations, and Gordy had memorized several of the catchy jingles from the television commercials. Any normal passerby may have raised an eyebrow at the amount of security needed to protect a multi-level marketing corporation, but while Somnium's products were real and beneficial, Gordy knew that it was all just a cover for the truth.

Behind the closed doors of that impregnable fortress was B.R.E.W. Headquarters. The Board of Ruling Elixirists Worldwide was the governing body of the potion community. The B.R.E.W. Chamber of Directors determined what potions could be concocted and which ones were in violation of the laws. Every legal advancement in potion making in the last thirty years had come from within the walls of B.R.E.W. Headquarters.

Goosebumps prickled on Gordy's arms. He was finally going to see where the magic happened.

Gordy's mom parked the van, and the two entered through the lobby doors. There was yet another security post. This time they had to empty their pockets and walk through an X-raying machine similar to the ones Gordy had seen at airports. Wanda carried all sorts of vials and ampoules in her purse, but they slid through the machine just fine.

A crystal chandelier dangled from the center of the ceiling directly above a desk where a receptionist issued Gordy a visitor's badge. He attached it next to his security clearance badge.

"Surprised to see you here today, Wanda," a man said, approaching from behind Gordy.

"Bolter?" Gordy's mom replied in surprise. "I could say the same thing about you. Don't you have business up North?"

"Indeed I do. But when the Chamber beckons, I must report. I'm showcasing my newest invention."

Bolter had dark skin and long black hair that draped down below his shoulders. He was incredibly tall and thin, towering above Gordy and his mom like an odd lamppost, only one with a pair of charcoal-colored goggles strapped to his forehead. He was also wearing jeans, which made his legs look ridiculously long. His eyes seemed to sparkle when he smiled. When he leaned forward to speak to Wanda, cupping his hands over his mouth, Gordy noticed Bolter was missing his fingers. With the exception of his thumbs, only gnarled stubs remained.

Bolter whispered something secretive to Wanda, and she reared back in surprise.

"You're kidding me! And they approved?" she asked, sounding impressed.

"Yes, indeedy! I just need to provide documentation." Bolter turned to face Gordy. "Who do we have here? An intern perhaps? One of B.R.E.W.'s youngest and finest?" His nose twitched, but then he placed a hand on Wanda's shoulder. "No! Don't tell me. Is this *the* Gordy Stitser?"

Gordy's mom nodded. "I had to bring him here to introduce you two eventually, didn't I?"

"I was beginning to think it would never happen." Bolter closed his eyes and bowed to Gordy. "Your mother tells me you have quite the gift. May I test your abilities?" The peculiar man reached into his front pocket and pulled out a small jar containing a white substance. Unscrewing the lid—an impressive skill, considering his lack of dig-its—Bolter mystically wafted his hand over the opening of the jar. "Yes, yes, go on. What do you sense?" he coaxed.

Gordy leaned forward and sucked in a deep breath, but it took only a second to decipher. "It's mayonnaise," he said, slightly confused.

Bolter's mouth fell open in a gasp. "So gifted!"

The corners of Gordy's lips lifted into a smirk as he glanced at his mom. "Gifted? That's a jar of mayonnaise."

"Delicious. Would you like some?" Bolter offered the jar.

Gordy politely declined.

Bolter clapped his nubs together. "So, are we touring the vicinity this morning?"

"Would you like to tag along?" Wanda asked, winking at Gordy.

Bolter glanced down at his watch, pursing his lips to-gether. "I have a few half hours I can thread together to show this young Dram the ropes."

───

Bolter had endless stamina, his tone lively and his man-nerisms animated, as he spouted off information like a ma-chine gun. He walked with a pronounced skip in his step, his thin legs swishing across the marbled floor, and he in-sisted on taking the stairs as well, sometimes three or four steps at a time. Gordy and his mom labored to keep up.

Each of the floors of B.R.E.W. Headquarters served

a different purpose. Bolter called them the four *M*s: Management, Military, Machinery, and Medical.

"We won't spend a lot of time on the first level," Bolter said. "Management. Administrative and legal operations. All sorts of boring and blahs." He winked at Gordy. "Though your mother would like to have a corner office on this floor one day."

"I would," she agreed. "That would mean less travel. More family time."

Bolter made a disgusted face. "Such a waste of talent, if you ask me." He bent over to address Gordy at close range. "Wanda has no doubt neglected to share with you this nugget of knowledge, but she is one of the greatest Elixirists in the world."

Gordy's mom burst out with laughter. "I don't like to lie to my children."

"But it's true," Bolter said, waggling his eyebrows. "She brews with vibrancy and revolutionary skill. Don't let her fool you, young Stitser. Wanda is one of the elite."

Gordy smiled and looked at his mom, who promptly shook her head in denial. It was nice to hear what other people thought of her abilities. She kept things close to the chest. He always wondered why she insisted on being so secretive.

"Ah, floor two." Bolter waved a magnetic badge over a sensor. "Military."

A door opened, revealing more security guards studying the Stitsers as they entered. A hallway of doors stretched out in front of Gordy. Various placards displaying names and specifications were adhered to the lintels. Gordy read a few of the signs as he passed.

CHARLES CAPSIC—WEAPON ENHANCEMENTS
ISAIAH GOVINE—BALLISTICS
ZELDA MORPHATA—EXPLOSIVES

Gordy smirked. "I didn't know there were so many Elixirists involved in the military. What does potion making have to do with war?"

Bolter sighed. "It has everything to do with it, unfortunately. Weapons are one of the areas where we Elixirists naturally excel. Shame. So much damage can be done by one tiny vial. Ask Einstein. He knew all too well about the dangers of revealing one's talent."

"Einstein was an Elixirist?" Gordy asked.

Bolter gawked at Gordy's mom in shock. "What have you not told this boy?"

Wanda smiled and then nodded at one of the doors. "Is Zelda in the office today?"

Bolter clicked his tongue. "I thought she would be, but the lights are out." He jiggled the doorknob. "Door's locked. Perhaps she took a sick day?"

"Can we see inside any of these offices?" Gordy asked. He wondered what sort of workstations militarized Elixirists used. Did they have special cauldrons and ingredients?

"You know, I'd rather not linger too long on this floor,"

Gordy's mom said. "A lot of these folks aren't as pleasant to converse with as Bolter is. Has to do with their line of work, I suppose."

They climbed the next flight of stairs, huffing and puffing and clinging to the handrail, though Bolter never showed any signs of being winded.

"Machinery!" Bolter cheered, bursting through the door with his arms outstretched. "Welcome to my humble abode."

There weren't any security guards roaming the hallway on this level. In fact, the whole floor felt empty, as if the three of them were the only living beings around.

Gordy scrunched his nose, but before he could ask why any Elixirist would need to meddle with machinery, Bolter drew their attention to the opened door near the center of the hallway. His name appeared on the placard above the door, though it could have been scribbled on with a permanent marker.

Bolter's office looked like an automotive junkyard. Bumpers, mufflers, and carburetors dangled from chains throughout the room. A mountain of rolled-up blueprints had been piled in one corner. Gordy spotted Stevia, Vietnamese coriander, and an enormous cluster of broccoli stalks hanging from an herb drying rack. Bunsen burners and a rusted steel cauldron were in the other corner. The floor was slick with oil, and the room smelled like diesel.

"This is where I find my inner peace," Bolter said, beaming. "What do you think, Gordy? Impressive?"

"Yeah," Gordy lied. How could Bolter work in such a disheveled lab? "So what is it you do exactly?"

Bolter blinked and grinned. "Isn't it obvious?"

Maybe it should have been obvious, but the office needed a serious overhaul, and the whole room made Gordy itch uncomfortably. Now he understood why his mom insisted on keeping their lab so orderly. It just made practical sense. How could anyone mix and brew in an environment so filled with chaos?

"Bolter works in automotive concoctions," Gordy's mom explained. "It's his primary responsibility at B.R.E.W."

Then it all became clear. The car parts. The oil. The hanging light fixture made entirely of headlights. "That's cool," Gordy said. "But what do you do with cars? Make them go faster?"

"Not exactly," Bolter said. "Volatile chemicals have a negative impact on emissions. On this floor, we try to cut down on pollution. Better for the environment. You understand?"

"I guess, but how?" Gordy nudged a tray of lug nuts, scattering them across the floor. Bolter never noticed, his unblinking eyes focused on Gordy's.

"Have you not heard of hybrid vehicles?" Bolter asked.

"You made those?" Gordy curled his lip, impressed.

Bolter started to nod, but then opted to shake his head instead. "Not exactly. But I know several members on the team that were involved in the hybrid program. And I may

have given them a gentle nudge here and there in the right direction."

Gordy's eyes widened. "Wait a minute." He pointed at Bolter. "Are you the one working on our Subaru?"

Bolter's grin faltered. "Oh, uh . . . yes, that's me."

No wonder their car had been out of commission for so long, if someone like Bolter had been meddling with it.

"Should be ready to go soon," Bolter insisted. "Just a few more days for the mixture to percolate in the gas tank."

Yeah, right, Gordy thought. And then what would happen? Would the Subaru implode?

A blaring car horn honked in the room, and Gordy covered his ears. The sound came from underneath a pile of hubcaps that Gordy realized was actually Bolter's desk.

"Your phone's ringing," Wanda said calmly.

Bolter glanced down at the phone, his eyebrows rising. "Ah, it's Zelda! She's come to work after all. Yes, I probably should take that," he said. "Would you like to unbury a seat or two and wait? I could show you some of my latest projects."

Wanda smiled at Gordy, and he silently pleaded with her to escape immediately. "I'm sure Gordy would love to hear all about them, but I have to get him back to school before lunch," she said. "And we still have a few more stops to make on this tour."

Gordy sighed with relief. Bolter was nice enough, but if given the choice, he would've rather listened to his dad talk about chest freezers for several hours than spend another minute in Bolter's disastrous office.

The horn honked again, and Gordy jumped. Bolter adroitly plucked the phone receiver from his desk with one fingerless hand and bowed his good-byes to Gordy and his mom.

CHAPTER

7

N ow, this is my office," Wanda announced after she had led Gordy to the fourth floor and through a plain wooden door.

A plastic plant teetered on one corner of her desk, along with a computer and about half a dozen binders. There was a filing cabinet as well, but that was it. No windows. The only picture was an old photo of the family posing beside the Alamo. The walls were gray and navy blue, and the office was neat and tidy.

"What do you think?" Wanda asked, plopping down into her swivel chair.

Gordy looked around the room. Where were the cauldrons? The beakers and flasks and paper packets of exotic herbs? How did his mom brew? Gordy had never understood what exactly his mom did for a living, but he had always assumed it involved medicine. She was constantly flying to conventions where she presented her various findings.

"I don't know," Gordy said, looking down at his shoes. "It's not what I expected."

"What did you expect?"

He shrugged. "Something a little less . . . normal."

His mom raised her eyebrows. "Something more magical?"

"Well, yeah." He didn't want to sound childish, but where was the mystery?

"Most of the offices here, aside from Bolter's of course, will be more in line with what you're looking for. But in truth, I'm not like the others who work on this floor. I may have a medical background, and work on side projects now and then, but those are hobbies really. I actually don't spend a lot of time in this office."

Gordy shifted his weight. "I know. You travel and speak at conferences."

She smiled. "Sometimes. I do travel, but not always to where you think."

Gordy frowned. If not to conventions or conferences, where did she go all the time? Over the past four years, ever since Gordy discovered the existence of B.R.E.W. and his mom's role at the headquarters, she had spent at least six months out of every year away from home. She was always on the road to places like Kansas and Delaware. Boring places where she showcased her findings on allergy remedies and whatnot.

"Come with me." Wanda stood up from her chair and came around her desk. She clasped Gordy's hand in hers and led him back to the elevators. "I want to show you something."

Once inside, his mom inserted a key in the elevator's control panel and pressed a red button that appeared below the numbered floors. The gears whirred and creaked as the elevator descended past the bottom floor and lower parking levels. Finally, the elevator arrived at its destination. The doors slid apart, and Gordy stepped out into a brightly lit hallway. The light, however, did not come from lamps or chandeliers like the one in the main lobby. Instead, an unusual silver light emitted from inside a glass room up ahead.

There was another security post with an X-ray machine and multiple armed guards standing watch in front of the room. One of the guards nodded at Gordy's mom when she held up her security badge.

"You don't have access to go in," she said to Gordy, "but my badge is an all-access pass. It is linked to my body signature. Anyone trying to enter B.R.E.W. without security clearance would be arrested. That's why I had to file paperwork to have you cleared in order to accompany me today." Wanda nodded toward the glass room. "Anyone trying to enter there without this pass would face something much, much worse than imprisonment."

"Like what?" Gordy whispered.

"Death, for starters. If you're lucky." His mom grinned.

Gordy couldn't tell if she was being serious or not.

Something told him she was only half joking. "What's in there?"

"That room contains the Vessel." His mom pointed to a glowing chalice behind the glass. Resting on a crystal pedestal, the chalice looked like a large golfing trophy, with handles on either side, and a wide mouth filled with some sort of liquid. It was the liquid that glowed with the silver light, and Gordy marveled at its surprising brilliance. "It is the source of our power here at B.R.E.W. The Vessel grants authority to all members of the Board, including me." She rested her hand on Gordy's shoulder. "It's how we've been able to make such impressive developments in society. All of our medical findings, our weapons, and our technological advancements. Even Bolter's lonely floor of automotive improvements can be linked to the Vessel."

The potion inside the Vessel remained in a state of constant motion. Gordy wondered what made it move so much. The chalice wasn't resting on a cauldron or any heat source that he could see, nor was it hooked to a centrifuge. And yet the Vessel's contents never settled, the surface ceaselessly rippling.

"That potion is the most important one ever invented," Gordy's mom said. "Thus the reason for such heightened security. It needs to be protected."

"From who?" Gordy wondered.

Wanda licked her lips and sighed. "Unfortunately, B.R.E.W. has its share of enemies."

That was news to Gordy. Enemies? Why would the potion-making world have enemies?

"As a member of B.R.E.W., I have certain rights and abilities to help maintain the peace in the potion community," his mom said. "That's what I really do. It's a secretive job, and so I have an office on the Medical floor that serves as a decoy."

Gordy's forehead furrowed. "Are you like a cop?" Was his mom trying to say she was in B.R.E.W. law enforcement?

"No, not a cop. More like a bounty hunter."

Gordy's mouth dropped open. "Serious?"

"I have the power to, if necessary, lock terrible people away. People who would use their gifts of potion making to cause harm to the innocent. The Vessel gives me the power to bind my judgments."

Gordy's stomach clenched into knots, and he felt a tremor in his fingers. His mom was sharing a secret about her alternate life, and he wasn't sure he was ready to hear about it. Gordy wasn't afraid of her, rather he was worried about the dangers she apparently faced whenever an early morning taxi whisked her away to the airport.

His mom squeezed his hand and took a deep breath. "I wasn't planning on going into great detail about it, but you've grown so much this past year. You're coming into your own and developing your gift. I felt you were ready to understand the truth about the world you live in."

"Does Dad know?"

She nodded. "Your father understands a lot of what I do, but even he doesn't know the extent of my responsibilities."

"So when you went to Topeka earlier this week . . ." Gordy started.

Wanda shook her head. "I can't go into details of my recent trip, but I can tell you I didn't go to Kansas. I'm sorry, Gordy, for the lies. I hope you understand that I wasn't able to tell you the truth because of the nature of my work. I just don't want you to be mad at me."

"I'm not mad at you." At least, Gordy didn't think he was mad. Discovering his mom's secret life was actually kind of cool. If anything it made her kind of like a superhero or someone like James Bond.

"Do you have any questions for me?" she asked.

Gordy nodded. "What's in it?"

She scrunched her nose in confusion.

"The Vessel?" Gordy pressed. "What ingredients are in it?"

"Aha! You want to test out your skills, do you? Well, don't even think about it, bucko! There are too many different variables and ingredients involved, concocted by the most skilled Elixirists ever to master a potion, for even a young Dram like you to Decipher it. But I can tell you it's really old." She gazed through the window, eyeing the Vessel with reverence. "The founders of B.R.E.W. created it almost three hundred years ago."

Gordy watched as the potion roiled and churned. A

silvery bubble formed at the surface and popped. His nostrils flared as he strained to catch a whiff of the mysterious mixture, but the glass was too thick and he couldn't pick up even the slightest of scents.

"So you hunt people?" Gordy asked, his voice strained. "Like you catch them and lock them away? Do they try to hurt you?"

"Not usually," she said. "I've had years of practice to perfect the art of sneaking up on them. Catching them unaware. Incapacitating them in a way that doesn't allow for retaliation." She winked at Gordy.

The elevator chimed, and the door opened behind them. Bolter swished in, his legs scrambling, his hand still somehow clutching the phone.

"Wanda!" Bolter shouted, blurring past a couple of guards who had leaped to their feet. Bolter looked panicked, his eyes wild and his hair ruffled. For the first time since Gordy had been introduced to him, Bolter looked out of breath.

"What is it?" Gordy's mom demanded.

Bolter squeezed the phone and held it away from him as though it were about to explode. "It's your sister," he said. "It's Priss."

Wanda snatched the phone from Bolter's hand and pressed it against her ear.

"Hello?" She reared back as the piercing sound of static erupted from the receiver. "Priss? What's happened? What have you done?"

Gordy swallowed. He had never heard his mom so angry at his aunt before. Gordy loved Aunt Priss. She was always sneaking him secret ingredients to practice with or sending him special packages. It had been more than a year since he saw her last. Why was his mom shouting?

"No. You come in, now!" his mom bellowed. "Priss, I can't hear you. What are you talking about?" And then the static stopped. Wanda stared at the phone, and Gordy knew the line had disconnected. His mom looked at Bolter, her jaw clenching in anger.

"Wanda, I heard very little," Bolter said, "but I did hear her say Chicxulub."

Gordy's mom nodded. "I know," she muttered.

Gordy didn't dare ask the meaning of the unusual word. It didn't sound like an herb or an ingredient to any potion he had ever heard about. But he could sense from his mom's behavior that now was not the time to ask questions. She motioned for him to follow her, and the three of them silently rode the elevator up to the main level.

So, where is your mom, anyway?" Max asked, slumped on a stool in the Stitser lab.

Gordy glanced up from his workstation and caught himself before he blurted out the truth. "Oh, she's at a conference or something. I don't know."

It was hard having two close friends who knew a little of the Elixirist world and not be able to share all of his secrets with them. Max and Adilene knew Gordy's mom was a skilled potionist who used her talents for her position at Somnium. Her job sent her frequently out of town to sell lotions and body care products. Somnium Fine Creams and Oils had a reputation for being mysterious in their production methods, so owning a lab with a variety of weird herbs and ingredients wasn't that far-fetched if your mom was a successful Somnium salesperson. Of course, Max and Adilene had no clue about the existence of B.R.E.W., and Gordy's mom insisted it remained that way.

After the strange phone conversation at B.R.E.W.

Headquarters, Gordy's mom had been distracted, her thoughts preoccupied on something else. She dropped him off at school and then sped away. When Gordy arrived home directly after school, he had just enough time to give his mom a hug, ask permission to allow his friends into the lab—which she agreed to without batting an eye—and say good-bye before she hopped in a taxi and headed for the airport. Her destination was a mystery. Even his dad seemed unsure of where she was headed.

As soon as Max and Adilene arrived, Gordy buried his head in one of his mom's exotic herb manuals, searching for any clues to the meaning of Chicxulub. Where did it come from? What was it? A plant? An animal? So far, he hadn't found any hint to its meaning.

Max drummed his fingers on a yellow tin box. "What's Kyckling Snor?" he asked. He pointed to the faded writing scribbled on a piece of masking tape stuck to the box's rusted lid.

Gordy grimaced. "Uh, it's probably better that you don't know."

"Say that word again, Gordy," Adilene said, digging in her pocket and producing her cell phone.

"Kyckling Snor?" Gordy asked, glancing up from his book.

"No, not that one. The one you're looking for," she said.

"It's Chicxulub, I think. But I might be saying it wrong."

If only Gordy knew the word's etymology. Most ingredients derived their names from their country's origin or from where the item could be found most prominently in the wild. Just like the box containing Kyckling Snor. While normal chicken snot was never a welcomed ingredient, the Swedish variety played an essential role in creating a high-performing transparency potion. A few years ago, Gordy had used the sticky substance in order to see through the wrapping paper of his Christmas presents.

"Could we mix something already?" Max begged. "We've been down here forever!"

"Sorry," Gordy said, closing his mother's herb manual. "I'm just trying to figure something out."

"Well, figure out how to grow plants out of Mr. Boone's armpit, or something," Max said. "That would be more productive. And it would get me out of my World History exam tomorrow." He chuckled, the smell of corn chips on his breath, as he mimicked raising his hand in class. "Excuse me, Mr. Boone. Could we please be done with this test now? You're sprouting!"

"I knew it!" Adilene shook her phone triumphantly, causing Max to nearly topple from his stool. "I knew I had heard of that place before. Chicxulub, Mexico. I learned about it when I lived in El Salvador."

"You learned about what?" Max steadied his stool and glared at Adilene.

"About the asteroid," she said, showing the screen image to Gordy. "It's what ended the dinosaurs. Supposedly." Adilene made air quotes with her fingers. "It says here that the Chicxulub Asteroid made impact about sixty-six million years ago."

"It's a place?" Gordy gently placed a couple of vials onto the counter and leaned over Adilene's shoulder. "I didn't even think of that."

"So what do dinosaurs have to do with it?" Max asked, cramming a handful of corn chips into his mouth.

"Probably nothing," Gordy said. "But an impact crater could be a prime location for harvesting hazardous ingredients." He rushed over to a filing cabinet near the rear of the lab and rummaged for a moment in the top drawer. When he returned to the counter, Gordy held a dusty, leather book with crinkled pages. "This is one of my mom's old resource manuals," he said, carefully flipping through the book until he discovered the chapter he was looking for.

CHAPTER EIGHT—ALCHEMICAL RUINS

The chapter contained several pages of geological locations throughout the world noted by the Elixirists for having an abundance of perilous ingredients. Gordy ran his finger down the list:

> Chernobyl, Ukraine
> Mayak, Russia
> Sellafield, United Kingdom
> Vredefort Crater, South Africa
> Sudbury, Ontario
> Manson, Iowa
> Antipodes Islands
> Palmyra Atoll

As he continued to scan, he felt his hopes deflate. Nowhere on the list did he see the name Chicxulub, Mexico. That could only mean one thing. If it wasn't included in his mom's manual, then the asteroid crater was not of any significance in the potion community.

Gordy sighed in frustration. "It's not here."

"So, does he have eyeballs and lips and stuff?" Max asked.

"Huh?" Gordy looked up from the manual and saw Max hovering over Bawdry's body bag. "Oh"—he shook his head—"I don't think so. And if he does, they're all shriveled up."

"Wicked! Like my grandpa." Max waggled his eyebrows. "He has some sort of lip fungus that makes him look like he's chewing with a pair of prunes. You should see him eat his morning grapefruit. It's unpleasant. Come on, Gordy! Let me borrow the gas mask just for a second to take a look."

Before Gordy could object, Max raced over to the counter and had nearly succeeded in laying claim to the coveted gas mask when Adilene stuck out her foot and tripped Max. The sound of clattering cauldrons echoed through the basement.

"What are you doing?" Gordy barely managed to rescue two of his mother's glass bottles before they would've met their shattery end on the floor.

"Adilene tripped me!" Max jabbed an accusatory finger in the girl's direction.

"It was an accident." Adilene said, but she didn't look particularly apologetic. "I didn't think you really wanted him to unzip Bawdry."

"He's off-limits, Max. Trust me, you don't want to see him," Gordy said.

Max stood and looked down at the wet splotches of ingredients soaking his shirt. "I'm covered in Kyckling Snor, and it—" His face contorted with fear. "It burns. It's burning me! I'm going to end up like Bawdry! You did this to me, Rivera. I think I'm melting!"

Gordy slapped his hands down on Max's shoulders and shook him. "It's lemon juice."

"I knew it!" Max writhed in agony. "The worst . . . I'm . . . Lemon juice?"

"Nice one, Maxwell." Adilene shook her head. "Do you always quote *The Wizard of Oz* when you freak out?"

"What are you guys doing down here?" Isaac stood in the doorway, looking at the mess the three twelve-year-olds had created.

"Isaac, you know the rules," Gordy said, startled by the appearance of his younger brother. "You're too young to be down in the lab."

"I know," Isaac said. "But I was yelling your name, and you didn't answer the door. Someone dropped off a package for Mom, and then drove away in a big brown truck." Isaac pointed a finger at Max's jersey. "You've got pee all over you."

"It's lemon juice." Max pretended to threaten Isaac with one of his fists, but the younger boy just shrugged.

"A package?" Gordy asked. "Like, as in a mailed package?"

Occasionally, his dad would receive weird toaster gizmos or faucets, but the packages his mom received always held much cooler stuff.

Gordy raced up the stairs, three at a time.

The musty brown package was no bigger than a shoebox and looked insignificant tucked underneath the corner of the welcome mat. Gordy felt let down by its smallness. Still, the handwriting unmistakably belonged to his Aunt Priss, which meant it could contain something extraordinary. There were a number of smudgy stickers adhered to all four sides of the box, listing the many countries and nations it had passed through before arriving at its destination.

Max crinkled his brow. "Who's Priscilla Rook?"

"She's my aunt. The one I told you about," Gordy said, hefting the box.

Max's eyes widened. "The crazy one who shrinks heads? Open it!"

The shrunken head accusation had never been proven, but Gordy refused to doubt his aunt's abilities.

"First, I have to test it." Gordy knew the drill. Taking the box back to the basement lab, he pulled a Ziploc bag filled with pink powder from one of the drawers of the apothecary tables.

"Hang on," Adilene said. "Won't your mom be upset if you open her stuff?"

Gordy sprinkled the powder on the package. The grains peppered the brown paper, but that was it. No sparks or electricity. No fizzing reaction.

"It's clean." Gordy gave an affirming nod. "But you're right. I don't think I better open it without my mom." After all, opening his mother's mail without permission could get him into a lot of trouble. Who knew what Aunt Priss had sent?

"Good idea," Adilene said. "What if it's full of bad stuff? Like poison?"

"Why would Gordy's aunt send him poison?" Max asked.

Adilene folded her arms. "She didn't send the package to *him*. She sent it to his mother."

"They're sisters," Max said. "They're not enemies. Gordy's aunt wouldn't send radioactive goop for no good reason."

Gordy nodded, but then he swallowed, considering the situation. From the part of the phone conversation he'd overheard between his mom and his aunt, it sounded like Aunt Priss was in trouble, which meant the package could have something important in it. Something that only the few people she trusted were meant to see. He also remembered all the things his mom had told him the day before. About the bad people she had to hunt down and catch. Dangerous people. Dark Elixirists who could potentially cause her harm. What if Aunt Priss's package had something to do with those sorts of people? What if his mom needed what was inside the box right now?

Without a second's hesitation, Gordy tore off the wrapper and removed the tape.

"I thought you were going to wait." Adilene slapped Gordy's shoulder with the back of her hand.

Remembering rule number one of the Five Rules of Potion Making—*Never draw unnecessary attention to the potion community*—Gordy didn't know how to easily explain himself.

"Uh . . . there could be ingredients that need refrigeration," Gordy reasoned. "I wouldn't want them to spoil."

"Yeah, Rivera!" Max added. "Mind your own business. What do you think is in it?" He rubbed his hands together in excitement, and though she frowned in disapproval, Adilene crowded behind Gordy as he opened the package.

Inside, Gordy first discovered a pair of 3XL turquoise sweatpants with an elastic band. The pants were pocked with holes and covered with mildew stains. He picked them up delicately, holding them by the waistband with his thumbs and forefingers. The sweatpants would have smothered his petite-sized Aunt Priss.

Max smirked. "It looks like a clown suit."

"No offense, Gordy, but your aunt's kind of odd," Adilene said, her long black hair tumbling across Gordy's shoulder as she leaned forward.

Gordy knew sometimes the post office opened strange

packages to ensure the safety of the contents. Elixirists often added clothes as a way to throw people off from what really lay inside. Diving to the bottom, he found a wooden box with hinges and a brass keyhole. Trembling with excitement, Gordy removed the box from the package and placed it on the floor.

"Open it!" Max leaned in, crowding Gordy.

"It's locked." Gordy returned to the package and searched for any sort of key, but after a few seconds of rummaging, he came up empty-handed.

"Check the pants," Max instructed, nodding at the turquoise sweatpants.

Gordy grinned. "That actually makes sense." He checked in the front pocket, and there it was.

A brass key with a small, circular head.

A moment of uncertainty struck him as he debated whether or not he should open the box. But then the moment passed. There was no turning back now that he had the key.

The hinges creaked as the lid opened. Inside, Gordy found three objects: a folded piece of paper and two glass vials. One of the vials was no bigger than his pinkie finger and had a circular section of brown cork wedged in the opening. It was empty. The other vial was corked as well, but that one ballooned out at the bottom and contained a thick, cream-colored liquid.

Gordy knew better than to open the bottles blindly.

The paper was obviously his aunt's instructions and he carefully unfolded it.

Wanda,
    I did what I thought was best. I'll explain it all once I'm clear. I'm so sorry, but I had little choice. Get ready for a war.
                        Priss

"Ominous," Max whispered.

"Do you even know what that word means?" Adilene asked.

Max frowned.

"Um, guys . . ." Gordy turned the paper over, trying to find any other scribbled instructions, but other than the strange message, there were no other words. He stared at the two bottles. "I don't think I was supposed to open this."

"Huh? That's odd. It's not like I didn't tell you not too," Adilene said sarcastically.

"Chill out," Max said. "All we need to do is wrap the package back up. Your mom will never know." He stood and nudged the box with his foot, causing the two vials to clink together.

Gordy instinctively shot his hand out to steady the bottles, and his fingers touched the small, empty vial. Something sharp, protruding from the cork stopper, pricked him, and he recoiled in pain as a tiny hole appeared at the center of his pointer finger. The empty vial suddenly filled with a reddish liquid. Gordy stuck his finger in his mouth and sucked away the sting, but the pain only lasted for a second. When he looked at his finger again, he couldn't find any pinprick on his skin. Then, like the disappearing pinprick, the red liquid in the bottle vanished as well, leaving it empty once more.

"Oh, man, Gordy, I honestly didn't mean to bump that," Max muttered. "What just happened?" He looked queasy, and Gordy felt a shiver of uneasiness pass through him.

"Yeah, what kind of weird potion is that?" Adilene slid backwards on the ground, putting distance between her and the package.

"I don't know." Gordy didn't have much experience handling vanishing concoctions. His Aunt Priss, though, was an Elixirist who spent the majority of her time travelling through exotic and mysterious lands. She wasn't known to be an obedient rule-follower, which meant the potion could have easily contained something hazardous.

"Maybe we should clean up," Adilene suggested. "And I probably need to get home."

"Yeah, you probably do," Max agreed.

Adilene scowled. "We both do!"

Gordy didn't argue as the three of them returned the items to the box and covered it with the pair of sweatpants. He struggled to remove the image of the strange vial from his mind and the red liquid appearing before suddenly and mysteriously vanishing. It had looked a lot like blood.

He didn't know how he knew it, but something told Gordy the blood was his.

CHAPTER

9

Two miles southeast of Mont Forel, in Sermersooq, Greenland, Priscilla Rook stared at the sign protruding from a section of the barbwire fence. She shivered.

Mianersorit aput sisurtuq—Avalanche Danger
Tornassuk—Polar Bears
And . . .
Tizheruk—Snake Monsters

Greenlandic warnings such as these sufficiently deterred most of the locals from wandering too far beyond the fence. Who would want to be chased by polar bears or snake monsters while avoiding an avalanche?

But Priscilla knew the truth. The ground was firm and solid and unlikely to give way to an avalanche anytime soon. Most of the polar bears lived at least a hundred miles west of the barrier, and snake monsters were nothing more than a myth created to scare villagers away from something worse. Something they wouldn't understand.

Plumes of crystallized breath puffed from Priscilla's lips as she breathed on her special glasses. It may have been on the waning end of summer in northern Greenland with a bright yellow sun shining in the sky, but the temperature was only fifteen degrees Fahrenheit.

Priscilla loathed the cold. She could hardly brew anything in such nasty conditions. An Elixirist had no business in such a place. Bundled in the warmest yak-skin coat she could purchase on short notice, she wiped the fog from her glasses and placed them on her eyes.

The words on the wooden sign transformed into another message.

BE WARNED!
This is the Forbidden Zone of Mezzarix,
Scourge of Nations.

The same message was repeated on every sign across the icy mountainside.

The name *Mezzarix* sent an unpleasant tremble through Priscilla's shoulders. How long had he been trapped here? Twelve years? His anger would be severe by now. Mezzarix's land spanned for miles, but he could be anywhere. Watching. Doubt filled her thoughts as she looked upon the barbwire fence and took a careful step back. No doubt it would be Stained with something sinister. Did she have the supplies to cure Rot or Plague, two of Mezzarix's favorites?

"You can't do this, Priss!" she hissed under her breath. "What were you thinking?"

Above her, gray pillows of clouds moved slothfully across an equally gray sky, and she cinched her fur-lined hood close to her ears. They felt numb and achy as though she could pinch her lobes and they would plumb fall off. It would storm soon, like it always did, and the trail would become too treacherous to travel.

Since she spent most of her time alone thousands of miles south of Greenland in her quiet cottage in Portugal with few creatures to talk to other than a goat and an eel, Priscilla always spoke out loud to herself.

"Look at those clouds." She looked up and gnawed on her lower lip. "Do you want to get caught outside in a blizzard? The temperature's going to drop. You know this." She nodded in acknowledgment. The temperature would drop. She knew she had no choice but to continue on. Turning back was not an option.

Returning the glasses to her inner-coat pocket, Priscilla removed her ratty brown gloves and a leather pouch from her bag. She sprinkled pink detection powder across the rusted, brown barbs of the fence. The powder settled on the wire, but that was all. Had there been a Dire Substance infection, the grains would have jumped and popped like a Fourth of July sparkler. No reaction meant one of two things: either Mezzarix had never wandered to this particular spot or he wanted a safe path for wanderers to travel through in order to capture them.

Priscilla felt the second was most likely the truth, but there seemed to be an excellent chance Mezzarix was somewhere else on the property. Somewhere far from the fence. How could he possibly know the goings-on of every inch of the Forbidden Zone?

Stepping through a gap in the barbwire fence, her eyes in constant motion, Priscilla pulled the drawstring on the pouch tight, dropped it in her satchel, and snapped the clasp with her thumb. Taking a deep breath, she pressed forward just as heavier snow began to fall.

By the time the sun had descended beyond her sight, only clouds occupied the sky overhead, and the precipitation had transformed into a biting mixture of snow and sleet that snapped at her cheeks like a swarm of angry wasps. It had been so long since she'd been here, she couldn't remember the direct path to the cave, and she began to worry. Was she lost? If so, where would she stop along the trail to make camp? Where would she find good, dry timber for a fire? Her stomach gurgled, and she grimaced with annoyance.

"You had to eat all those berries, didn't you? Couldn't have saved some for dinner? No matter. There's bound to be—" She clamped her mouth closed in surprise as she finally spotted the trail slicing through the mountain.

Two familiar marks appeared on the eastern wall. Handprints—one belonging to her, the other to her sister. The paint had been bright red when they had marked the trailhead twelve years ago, but now it looked more like dried blood.

"This is it," she whispered as a wave of emotion swelled inside her chest.

She took a step forward, but sputtered to a stop when she heard the sound of toppling rocks behind her. Swallowing, Priscilla turned around.

Mezzarix stood about twenty yards from her on the path. His long mane of unkempt, white hair would've camouflaged his face against the snowy backdrop had it not been for the charcoal-gray streak flowing through it and his silver pointed beard. He wore black suit pants and a suit coat with wide lapels and a black buttoned-up shirt underneath.

And he was barefoot.

Struggling not to lose control, she tried to force the memories of the ceremony that had banished him to the mountains from her thoughts.

"Hello, Priscilla," Mezzarix purred. "Still talking to yourself? That's not accepted in society now, is it?"

Priscilla steadied her hands at her side, her chest pounding with fear. "Hello, Father," she replied, unable to keep her voice from trembling.

It was Friday night, and Gordy sat at the dining room table, his chin smashed in his palms, eyeing his slice of pepperoni pizza going cold on his plate. Seated across from him, Gordy's dad had his face buried in the latest issue of *Royal Dishwasher Magazine*. Every so often, his dad would laugh at something he had read. Isaac was scarfing down his fourth slice of pizza while Jessica flicked bits of cheese across the table with her fingers.

"Stop that," Gordy muttered. He was the only one paying any attention to them.

Jessica gave him a crusty stare. "You're not in charge."

"Yeah, but Dad is," Gordy fired back, slightly more aggressive.

His dad snorted and said, "Heat-resistant drainage tubes. What a hoot!" Then he folded up the magazine and set it aside. "All right, you guys, what's up? Why's everyone all rattled?"

"I want a salad," Jessica whined. "I hate pizza."

"Who hates pizza?" Mr. Stitser leaned across the table and peeled a pepperoni off Jessica's untouched slice. He popped the piece of greasy meat into his mouth. "Every kid likes pizza, and your mother hardly ever serves it for dinner."

"And when she does, she usually hides fur and eyeballs and stuff in the sauce," added Isaac.

"Exactly." Gordy's dad pointed at Isaac. "I would've thought I'd be praised for ordering out, but the only one of you guys enjoying themselves is Isaac."

Isaac belched and nodded.

"What's wrong, Gordo? You feeling sick?" His dad gave him a concerned look.

"When's Mom getting back?" Gordy asked. Gordy's mom had yet to check in, and it had been close to twenty-four hours since she left hurriedly on an airplane. No one knew where she was going, at least Gordy didn't think his dad knew. It was possible his dad was just keeping tight-lipped on the matter.

His dad shrugged. "She didn't give an exact date. A week, maybe."

"A week?" Gordy couldn't remember a time when his mom spent more than a couple of days out of town. How was he supposed to wait that long to find out what was in Aunt Priss's package? The more he thought about it, the more it caused his stomach to twist. Gordy sighed. "May I be excused?"

"Of course," his dad said, and Gordy slid out of his chair.

"May I be excused, too?" Jessica widened her eyes with hope.

"Not until you finish your dinner."

"But, Dad, what about Gordy? He hasn't eaten anything either."

"She makes a valid point, Gordo." Mr. Stitser nodded at Gordy's plate.

Glaring at his sister, Gordy snatched the cold slice of pizza and crammed the entire piece into his mouth. "Happy?" he asked, which actually sounded more like "Abee?"

Jessica slouched in her chair, frowning as Gordy left the kitchen, noisily munching his meal.

⌒

Gordy's secret hiding spot lay beneath a two-foot-square section of carpet on his closet floor. The carpet's weblike design meant that anyone looking at the floor would easily miss it, including his parents, though he suspected his mom knew of its existence.

Upon pulling back the carpet, a loose board gave Gordy access to a fairly deep compartment underneath. He couldn't hide everything he wished to within the hole, but it was large enough to house a number of his possessions. A narrow wooden crate held nearly a dozen corked glass vials of liquid. The bottles contained different colored substances, some thin and watery, others dense and gloppy. These were his most dangerous potions, ones his mom might raise a fuss over.

Gordy had labeled each vial with a section of masking tape. RAT MAGNET. THE BALD-ERATOR. ROCKET VOMIT. One of the labels had the words EXTRA LIMB written on the tape. That dark purple potion would cause an additional appendage to suddenly appear on whoever drank from the vial. There was only one problem with it. Gordy had only tested it out on cockroaches. He wasn't exactly sure what sort of appendage would grow or where it would grow from.

Lying next to the crate of vials was Gordy's potion journal. It had a squishy brown leather cover and an elastic band, stretching from the back, which attached to a small brass knob on the top, keeping the journal closed tight. Every night, Gordy would sneak into his closet, pull out his journal, and jot down the ingredients needed to create the potions he had thought up during the day. From his last count, he had logged almost three hundred and fifty unique potions. It wouldn't be long before he would need a new journal.

Aside from the potions and his journal, Gordy usually kept only one other item of importance in the hiding place. He stared down at a black-and-white photograph of two young girls, probably close to Gordy's age. Both of the girls were holding a prize in their hands. The girl on the left held a severed lizard's tail like it was some sort of ribbon.

The girl on the right, who was at least a foot shorter than the other, held an enormous leg bone. The two girls were Gordy's mother, Wanda, and his Aunt Priscilla.

Standing behind them was an older man with long dark hair, pointy eyebrows, and a scruffy beard. It was the only picture Gordy had of his Grandpa Rook, who had spent most of his years toiling as a potato farmer in Northern Idaho. He had died just before Gordy was born.

Before he covered up the hole with the floorboard, Gordy glanced sideways and sighed as he examined Aunt Priss's package. He couldn't just leave it downstairs, unprotected. There were too many questions surrounding the mysterious box. He hoped his mom would understand.

Gordy hoisted the package out of the hole, sat down on his bed, and unfolded the note from his aunt.

Wanda,
  I did what I thought was best. I'll explain it all once I'm clear. I'm so sorry, but I had little choice. Get ready for a war.
      Priss

"'Get ready for a war'?" he whispered. An actual war? Or was it some sort of code only an elite Elixirist like his mother would understand?

Rubbing his fingers together, Gordy picked up the smallest vial, taking extra care not to touch the cork stopper. He examined it in the light and flicked the glass with his fingernail. The bottle looked completely empty. Maybe he had imagined the appearance of the bloodlike liquid, but Gordy didn't believe it. He ran his thumb over the spot where the bottle had pierced his finger and recalled the sudden pinprick.

"This is stupid," he muttered. His Aunt Priss may be mischievous, but she wasn't careless. She would have known Gordy might get to the package first. And nothing had happened to him since the vial pricked him. No weird formation of boils or third eyeballs.

Gordy exhaled slowly as he turned his attention to the bottle containing the cream-colored potion. He knew he should wait for his mom to come home, but curiosity propelled him to continue. He swirled the potion in the vial, and the liquid sparkled like the inside of a seashell. He shook the vial to agitate the potion, but the contents only glopped back and forth like thick slime. Gordy pinched the cork between his thumb and finger and twisted until it slid free. Bringing the opening up to his nose, he breathed deeply. The smell was dull, odorless, and indescribable. He furrowed his brow in concentration, taking a deeper breath.

But Gordy couldn't detect anything. Not a distinct herb or chemical or the faintest hint of an ingredient. Gordy's mom had once tested his ability with fifty different potions, ones he had never smelled before, and he had only missed identifying a handful of ingredients, and most of those were insignificant amounts within the potions.

And yet, despite his Deciphering skill, there was nothing unique within that bottle.

The doorbell rang downstairs. After a few seconds, Gordy could hear his siblings squabbling over who got to open the door as they raced down the stairs and slid across the floor. Still seated on his bed, Gordy recorked the vial and placed it carefully into the small box. He listened as Isaac undid the dead bolt and the security chain and opened the door.

"Hello," came a woman's soft voice. "Is your mommy or daddy home?"

"My dad's home. My mom's far, far away," Isaac replied.

"Really?" the voice inquired. "Did she just leave this evening?"

"Yesterday. She left on an airplane."

"Oh, how nice. Where did your mother go?"

Gordy scrunched his eyebrows and got to his feet. Why was this woman interested in his mother's whereabouts? He stepped into the hallway and craned his neck to peer down the stairs. A woman wearing a dark red pantsuit and high heels stood on the porch. Isaac had pulled the door wide, giving her a full view of the entryway. She wore thin glasses and had short, spiky blonde hair. In her left hand, she held a brown leather bag. Standing behind the woman was a middle-aged man with gray hair and a beard, wearing a sport coat and a floral tie.

Gordy's dad appeared from the living room and pulled Isaac from the doorway. "May I help you?" he asked.

The woman grinned warmly. "I hope so." With a flick of her wrist, she produced a white business card. "Esmeralda Faustus. Attorney at Law." She spoke with a British accent, and it reminded Gordy of one of the television shows his parents liked to watch on Sunday evenings. "This is my associate, Yeltzin."

Gordy's dad examined the card, turning it over in his hands to read both sides. "Ah, very good. And what can I do for you, Ms. Faustus?"

"Please, I prefer Esmeralda. You may keep that," she said when Mr. Stitser tried to return the card to her.

"Thank you." Mr. Stitser attempted to place the card into his pants pocket.

"Well, if you're not going to take care of it, you might as well give it back." Ms. Faustus snapped her fingers.

"Take care of what?" Gordy's dad asked, looking baffled.

"You'll just forget about it and end up washing those pants and ruining it. It's a waste of good credentials; ask anyone in the professional world."

"Oh, I apologize." Gordy's dad quickly removed his wallet from his back pocket and inserted the card into one of the slots. "Is that better?"

Ms. Faustus smiled evenly. "It's Gordon Stitser, correct? Gordon, I represent several clients who are deeply concerned and have voiced formal complaints with the

Department of Health and Safety." She ran her thumb down the edge of the door and stared at the smudge with a faint look of disgust.

Mr. Stitser flinched. "Formal complaints about us?"

"Indeed." She rubbed her smudged thumb and forefinger together. "Improper emissions, careless disposal of dangerous wastes, tendering of unregistered and, in many cases, banned plants and substances." She snapped her fingers at Yeltzin, who produced a piece of paper from his sports coat pocket and handed it to Ms. Faustus. "All charges are included in this affidavit," she continued. "Do you have a garden, by chance? A greenhouse?"

Gordy's dad didn't answer as he glanced at the page.

"Have you or your wife spent any recent time abroad, and within that time have you purchased any fruit, vegetables, or animals?"

"I don't . . . I don't think so. I mean we went to Canada last year, but only over the border to Niagara Falls. I . . . I . . . have some Canadian money."

That, of course, was a lie. Gordy's mom always brought home suitcases filled with exotic, growing things from her travels. If the Department of Health and Safety could have seen inside just one of Mrs. Stitser's carry-ons, the whole family could very well be arrested.

"Do you mind if we come in?" Esmeralda asked suddenly.

"Don't let them in, Dad!" Gordy whispered under his breath, hoping somehow the idea to turn the woman away would pop into his dad's head. There was something wrong about the well-dressed attorney and her shifty associate, Yeltzin.

"It is a bit chilly out tonight. We won't stay long." Esmeralda made a pouty face with puckered lips.

"I . . . I suppose you could come in for a moment," Gordy's dad conceded. "I'm still not quite sure what this—"

"Good. Thank you," she replied before he could finish his sentence.

Gordy watched Esmeralda step slowly into the entryway, her eyes darting about the room. For a brief second, she looked hesitant, almost worried, but then she smiled at Yeltzin and nodded. The gray-haired man stepped across the threshold. It was then that Esmeralda noticed Gordy lurking in the shadows upstairs.

"Hello," she called out to Gordy, beaming.

Gordy's back thudded against the wall as he tried to vanish.

"Now, now, I can see you," she chirped. "Come on down. Don't be shy."

Reluctantly, Gordy walked down the stairs and stood next to his father.

Ms. Faustus squinted as she stared at him. "Your name's Gordon, isn't it? Like your father. However, you don't go by Gordon, do you? And you're twelve years old. A bit short for your age, but twelve nonetheless."

Gordy's eyes narrowed in suspicion. How did she know about him?

She waved her hand dismissively. "I can tell these things. It's my job to be perceptive." Esmeralda returned her attention to Gordy's dad. "You have a lovely home, Mr. Stitser. Well decorated. So this is the landing and there's the living room, dining room, and in the back would be the kitchen, correct?" She pointed to the different locations on the first floor of the Stitser home.

"That's right." Gordy's dad sounded impressed.

"From our recent perusal of your floor plan, and judging by the windows outside, your second level has three bedrooms and two baths." Esmeralda licked her lips and removed her glasses long enough to clear an invisible blemish from one of the lenses. "Mr. Stitser, I understand your wife, Wanda, has left town."

Gordy's dad nodded. "Yes, she's away on a business trip."

"Will she be home soon? I apologize if I come across as nosy, but what we have to discuss concerns both of you, I'm afraid."

"Yeah, about that. Who made these formal charges?"

"Until we've completed a thorough investigation of the property, the identities of my clients must remain anonymous." Esmeralda tapped her toe against the hardwood floor and cocked her head, listening. She walked toward the living room, pausing every two or three steps to tap her foot.

Yeltzin followed, mimicking her actions by stomping on the floor.

As they disappeared into the next room, Gordy grabbed his dad's arm. "Why is she here? She's going to find out about mom's stuff. You need to make her leave!"

"Such manners," Esmeralda called out from the next room. "I take it your son has seen his share of discipline over the years. And if he hasn't, if he chooses to maintain that level of disrespect for authority, he shall."

Gordy's eyes widened in shock. No way his dad would let some stranger talk to him like that. For sure he would show the shifty woman the door.

"He's just had a bad day. Lots of stress. Haven't you, Gordy?" His dad leaned close and lowered his voice. "You need to relax. I'm curious to get to the bottom of these charges, and you aren't helping by being rude."

"What?" Gordy's mouth dropped open. How was he being rude?

Gordy heard the distinct sound of a doorknob jiggling. It was coming from the kitchen. Where the door was that led into the Stitser lab.

"Where does this lead?" Esmeralda asked. "A basement? Storage, perhaps?"

"Uh . . ." Mr. Stitser rushed into the kitchen, Gordy stepping on his heels. They found Ms. Faustus with her arms folded and Yeltzin twisting the doorknob with an alarming amount of force.

"That's our office," Gordy's dad explained.

"Why is it locked?" Yeltzin asked. One of his bushy eyebrows shifted into a sharp peak.

"Dad," Gordy urged, gritting his teeth. "Do something."

"You know what? I think it's time for you two to leave," Gordy's dad said, though his voice held some hesitation. "Until you have legal proof that you're allowed to be here to conduct any sort of investigation, I'm going to need to consult with a lawyer before allowing you back."

Esmeralda pursed her lips together and squeezed her slender, manicured fingers into two tight fists. "As you wish." She nodded at Yeltzin, who released the doorknob. "We shall return tomorrow with proof."

The two of them hurried past Gordy and his dad, nearly knocking over Isaac and Jessica in the living room, before exiting the house completely, the door slamming behind them.

Like an enormous mouth eagerly waiting to chomp, Mezzarix's cave looked anything but inviting.

"You'll forgive me, I hope," Mezzarix said as he led Priscilla toward the opening. "Had I known you would be visiting I would've taken time to tidy up."

Torches ensconced on either side of the opening flickered in the surging wind.

"You couldn't have at least put in a door?" Priscilla asked.

"A door is so off-putting," he said. "Nothing says 'stay out' quite like a locked door. And I . . . well, I wouldn't want to send the wrong message. I love visitors."

Closing his hand around hers, Mezzarix led his daughter through the opening, and the mouth swallowed them up into blackness. The dark only lingered for a few moments before the old man cracked two stones together and sparks ignited in a pit near the center of the cave. Soon a fire burned, and the flames licked the bottom of a black kettle.

The ceiling towered at least thirty feet above. There were a few stalactites pointing down on an otherwise flat surface. As the warmth and light of the fire filled the cave, various items took shape. A table made from a long slab of stone. A bed set against the far wall with blankets strewn about and two matted pillows. A bookshelf with at least a dozen books stood next to it.

"Where on earth did you get those?" Priscilla asked, shocked to see Mezzarix's selection of reading material.

"Tsk, tsk. Not everyone fears snake monsters or avalanches. I've summoned help from time to time." With a swoop of his hand, he draped a blanket over Priscilla's shoulders. "Here. You're freezing."

Mezzarix hurried off, vanishing behind an enormous stalagmite jutting up from the floor like a fang. Priscilla could hear the soft clink of glass as her father procured some ingredient. She quietly dug into her bag and pulled out a small vial filled with clear liquid.

She pursed her lips together and shook the bottle. The mixture swirled and bubbled. Then all at once, a cylinder of red appeared in the vial. Priscilla caught her breath, then pressed the bottle to her lips and kissed it before returning it to her bag.

"You seem tense," Mezzarix said, returning with two porcelain cups and a teapot. He poured some steaming liquid into each cup. "Nothing a spot of tea can't cure."

Priscilla accepted the cup and blew across the steaming

brim. As she sipped, she recoiled and made a sour face. "You consider this *tea*?"

Mezzarix grinned and set down the tea tray. "Yes, well, not exactly. Hard to brew a good cup out here, you know. It's more like hot citrus water."

She swished the drink around in her mouth and shook her head. "That's not citrus either."

"Oh, all right. It's a skulking mushroom that sprouts along the cavern walls. But if you close your eyes and allow your imagination to stretch a bit, you can almost catch a hint of flavor."

"At least it's hot."

Mezzarix sniffed. "It has been twelve years without a letter or any correspondence from you. Crossing into a Forbidden Zone carries a severe punishment. I highly doubt you garnered permission from the Board."

Priscilla looked at her father, her chest rising quickly with each breath. "I don't know that I should talk to you about this until my sister arrives."

Mezzarix sloshed tea down the front of his suit. "Wanda's coming here? To my cave? Oh, this is rich! You've certainly stirred up a hornet's nest if you've managed to involve her."

Priscilla shook her head. "None of this was her doing, but I can't fix it without her, so she'll come. She's Lead Investigator of B.R.E.W, as you know."

Mezzarix's mouth dropped open slightly. "How could I have known that? Lead Investigator?" He scrunched his nose in disgust. "I always knew she would be the one who would join the Board. Well, I can't blame her for her ambition."

Priscilla heard the echoing sound of footsteps rising from somewhere deep within one of the adjoining caves. "Are you expecting company?" She stopped short as a skeleton ambled into the room.

Tall and slender, with bony arms and legs, the creature moved with almost comical footsteps, producing a *clickity-clack, clickity-clack* sound as it clambered over the rock ledge. Instead of a skull, a round egg-shaped stone had been attached to its neck with a long piece of moldy rope. Someone had drawn a face on the stone, which was stuck in a permanent smile.

Priscilla dug her hand into her leather satchel and pulled out a vial of sparkly, pistachio-colored liquid as the skeleton skittered to a halt a few yards from Mezzarix's cauldron.

"Priss, I would like to introduce you to Doll," Mezzarix said, nodding at the creature. "Doll, this is my daughter, Priscilla."

Doll stood motionless, the rock face not moving in the slightest to greet her.

Priscilla gasped. "Doll?"

"I was always terrible with names. Now, Doll, don't be rude. Say hello to Priscilla."

Doll's head tilted ever-so-slightly to one side.

"Wha . . . how?" Priscilla asked, retreating another step.

Mezzarix raised an eyebrow. "How did I make him? Are we sharing now? Secrets *are* meant to be shared."

She shook her head violently. "No! I don't care how you made it. Whose life did you take to create it?"

Priscilla knew this wasn't the first offense of Mezzarix using the dangerous potion of Risorgimento, or the reanimation of the dead. Before his banishment, the Scourge of Nations often violated that rule. He believed all inanimate or dead things were available for his control. She repressed a shudder.

Mezzarix scoffed. "I found the bones in one of the caverns a few years ago. Someone who met an unfortunate end. Must have been there for decades. I got rid of his skull, though. Didn't like the way he looked at me. Oh, come now! Stop staring at him as though he were some sort of monster."

"Your banishment should've prevented you from concocting such a powerful potion."

"Indeed. But time wears on everything, including banishments. Unfortunately, the strength of my command on Doll, as well as any other potion I brew, ends at the borders of the Forbidden Zone."

"This is insane. I shouldn't be here," Priscilla said.

"Don't be that way." Mezzarix sprinkled more ingredients into his cauldron. "The soup's almost ready, and you know I was only showing off. If it makes you feel better,

I will send Doll to harvest more skulking mushrooms. I'm almost out of tea."

Priscilla shivered as she watched the skeleton lurch away into the darker parts of the cavern, the rhythmic *clickity-clack* of its movements echoing throughout the cave.

"I should wait for Wanda somewhere else," she said. "She'll be here soon."

"I'm already here." Wanda stood in the opening of the cave, wearing a bulky, fur-lined parka with her hood pulled back revealing glaring eyes.

Eyes that remained glued to Mezzarix in the center of the room.

12

Gordy sat on a stool at the counter in Adilene's kitchen, while Adilene and her mother cooked *pupusas* on the stove. Flour splotched Adilene's caramel-colored skin as she flattened circular lumps of dough in her hands. The Riveras made *pupusas* at least once a week and sold them at the local Farmer's Market. Gordy insisted on being present because Mrs. Rivera always let him sample a few of her delectable creations, free of charge.

"You want first?" Adilene's mom asked, plopping a doughy patty on the paper plate in front of Gordy. Gordy's mouth watered as the scrumptious smell of seasoned beef and cheese filled his nostrils.

"Thank you, Mrs. Rivera," Gordy said.

The cheering chatter from a baseball game carried in from the next room where Mr. Rivera dozed in front of the television.

"So, what did she find?" Adilene asked. "This Ms.

Faustus? Do you think she suspects your mom of something?"

"It's hard to tell," Gordy said. "My dad finally kicked them out before they broke through the basement door. But my mom doesn't keep everything locked away in the lab." Though he didn't know for sure what constituted an invasion of privacy, he was positive Ms. Faustus's and Yeltzin's visit fell into that category.

"Why did she come to your house in the first place? Who made the complaints?" Adilene asked.

"I don't know," Gordy said. "It could've been the Judds. They're pretty nosy." The Judds were the elderly next-door neighbors. Mrs. Judd was pleasant enough, but her husband was quite the grump.

"Your mom does grow weird things in the yard. Someone must've finally noticed." Adilene dipped her fingers into the bowl of masa batter and brought up a handful, which she expertly formed into a patty. "I almost forgot. *Mi madre* told me something interesting about that asteroid crater in Chicxulub."

Adilene turned to her mother and asked her something in their native tongue. Gordy understood only a few words and simple phrases in Spanish. He tried to listen, but the two Riveras spoke way too fast to follow. For most of Gordy and Adilene's conversation, Mrs. Rivera seemed to pay no attention.

When they were finished conversing, Adilene turned

back to Gordy. "She said that the entire crater gives off a magnetic field."

Gordy crinkled his brow. "Really?"

"Yeah. Airplanes have to fly around the area because the energy causes their instruments to fail."

Gordy bit into his *pupusa*, the warm bread dissolving like butter in his mouth. He wasn't sure if a magnetic field had anything to do with his mom's connection with Chicxulub. It was possible that all asteroid craters gave off similar energy, and as far as he knew, magnetism didn't play much of a role in potion making.

Gordy's phone buzzed as a call came through. It was from his dad.

"Hey, Gordo! I'm taking the twins to the store to get some water filters. Then I'll probably pick up Chinese food for dinner. Sound good?"

"Sure," Gordy said. "Could you get another can of air freshener for Bawdry?" The mummy had gone two days without a good spray, and the toxic smell was about to breach the basement door.

"Already done," his dad answered. "Picked up a can this morning. Ocean Breeze. That should be a nice change. You see, son, I may not have the skills like you and your mother, but I have a few tricks up my sleeve. That reminds me, you haven't signed for any packages lately, have you?"

Gordy swallowed. He glanced over at Adilene and her mom, but they were too busy making another batch of *pupusas* to notice his worried expression. "Uh, no, I don't think so," Gordy said. "Why?"

"No reason. Just checking. I'll be back in an hour with dinner." Mr. Stitser hung up.

Gordy wanted to throw up. Why had he lied to his dad? He had never done that before, at least, not on purpose. But something had felt wrong about his dad's question. And truthfully, Gordy hadn't signed for anything. The delivery man had left the package on the front porch before driving off.

Gordy suddenly bolted off the stool. "Do you want to come over to my house?" he asked Adilene. Now more than ever, Gordy had to know what Aunt Priss's vials contained. Too much mystery had built up around them, and he needed to discover if they were dangerous potions or not. Especially since Gordy's mom had been gone for two days and had yet to check in.

Adilene's hands were sticky with masa. "What's wrong?"

"I need to check something . . . downstairs." He raised his eyebrows and Adilene gave a knowing look.

She turned to her mother, but Mrs. Rivera was already grabbing the ball of mixture away from her.

"It's okay," her mom said. "I will finish."

"We don't have a ton of time before my dad gets home," Gordy said as he and Adilene hurriedly raced across the street.

"What are we doing?" Adilene asked, breathing heavily as they ran.

"I need to test something in the lab. Just to make sure . . ." Gordy plowed face-first into Max who had been hiding behind the bushes next to the Stitsers' porch. Gordy reared back in surprise, clutching his chest and plopping on the ground with a thud.

"Ha!" Max shouted. "Totally scared you. You should have seen the look on your faces!"

"Maxwell, sometimes you don't think, do you?" Adilene helped Gordy to his feet.

"Yeah, well, at least I don't have dough in my hair." He started to chuckle, but then sputtered to a stop. "Wait a minute. Is that what I think it is? Is your mom making *pupusas*? Why wasn't I invited?" Max demanded.

"Because you were grounded for flunking your math exam," Adilene said. "Why aren't you in your room, studying?"

A mischievous grin cracked Max's lips. "I paid my dad off."

"You did what?"

Max snickered. "I gave him a bag of Cheetos from my personal stash. He was super hungry, so he decided to pardon me of my punishment. Cheesy snacks—it's the Pinkermans' undoing." He shook his head. "So, what's going on? Are we mixing a new potion? Something explosive?"

"I'm going to try something on the vials my Aunt Priss

sent. See if I can figure out what's in them." Gordy entered the house, headed for the kitchen, and was about to open the door into the basement when he remembered Bawdry and paused. Gordy turned and jumped back with surprise.

Max stood behind him, already with the gas mask fitted over his head.

"Pretty please, dude," Max said, reaching for the can of air freshener. "I really need to do this."

13

Wanda!" Priscilla gasped, whirling to face her sister.

"Oh, good!" Mezzarix cheered. "Just in time for dinner. Can I offer you a bowl of my world-famous Caribou Moss Stew?"

In response, Wanda hurled a bottle to the ground. The glass exploded upon impact, and a cloud of green smoke plumed up from the shattered remains, engulfing Mezzarix. He squirmed as a flurry of vines formed in the cloud and began tightening around his arms and legs, binding him to the ground. One of the greenish vines coiled over his mouth, preventing him from uttering a word. When the cloud of smoke dissipated, Mezzarix lay helplessly entwined on the hard stone floor, like a fly caught in a spider's web.

Wanda removed her gloves and turned on her sister. "You've crossed the line this time! I'm taking you to face the Board."

Priscilla dropped to the floor, cowering in the presence of her sister. "Let me explain. I . . . I did what I thought—"

"No!" Wanda boomed. "You don't get to explain yourself. Now where is it?"

Priscilla shook her head. "Where's what?"

With lightning speed, Wanda shot her hand into her satchel and produced another potion vial. "Don't think I won't offer you the same treatment as him"—her eyes flitted toward Mezzarix—"because I will. Now, give me the Eternity Elixir. I won't ask again."

Priscilla covered her mouth. "I don't understand. I sent it to you in a package."

"What package? There was no package."

"This can't be happening." Priss swallowed, and then held up her hands submissively. "It was a small parcel. I sent it a few days ago."

Wanda closed her eyes, lowering the potion to her side. "There haven't been any packages. At least none that I know of. Why did you take it?"

"I had no choice. A few months ago, I began associating with a new . . . friend." She dropped her eyes in shame. "A woman by the name of Esmeralda Faustus."

Wanda thought for a moment. "The name sounds familiar."

"I thought Esmeralda and I shared similar goals, but there was something about her. Maybe it was her views against the Board. Don't get me wrong. You know I'm not a fan of the governing laws of B.R.E.W., but Esmeralda was different. She absolutely hated the Board, and she was never truly my friend. It was all an act. Played out so I would let down my guard. And then she—she *Blotched* me." Priscilla shook her fist. "It was a simple Reveal All draught, and I told her everything. About the Eternity Elixir, and how we hid it in that asteroid crater in Mexico. When the Blotching effects wore off, Esmeralda was already on her way to dig it up. The only reason why she doesn't have it right now is because I found out in time to Blotch one of her employees and intercept the Elixir."

"If I may," Mezzarix said calmly. He had managed to work his mouth free from the vines and stared at Priscilla, an innocent grin on his lips. "I have to agree for once with Wanda. You really need to be wiser in your choices of friends, Priscilla. Esmeralda Faustus is a lunatic. Her parents were Dark Elixirists, a family of Scourges that rose to power forty years ago, when Esmeralda was just a preteen," Mezzarix explained. "If you had done your research, Priss, then you would've discovered the Faustuses were known throughout the potion community as being extremely skilled in Blotching. That's what they do. I should know; I taught her parents."

"Why does that not surprise me?" Wanda asked. "You were always involved with the wrong side."

"Yes, but I was never for absolute chaos."

"Ha! That's a new one," Priscilla said. "Killing all seven members of the Governing Board wasn't chaos?"

"I never killed anyone," Mezzarix said.

"Because we stopped you before you had the chance," Wanda muttered.

Mezzarix flexed his jaw. "There are many who agreed with me that B.R.E.W. was due for a change in command. New government. A reconstitution of the laws. More freedom for all. But let's not argue about something as trivial as my past transgressions. I'm not the topic of discussion here, am I? I thought we were discussing Esmeralda Faustus."

Wanda faced her sister. "What does she want with the Eternity Elixir, Priss?"

Priscilla sighed. "She plans to empty the Elixir into the Vessel."

Wanda narrowed her eyes. "Why would she do that?"

Mezzarix chuckled. "Now that's ambition. I take back what I said about Esmeralda. She's not a lunatic. She's a visionary."

"How do you figure?" Priscilla asked.

Mezzarix's laughter died off as he closed his eyes. "First, if you don't mind, Wanda, dear, my stew needs a little attention before it bubbles over." Steam rolled over the lip of the blackened cauldron. "Just a quick stir and then pull it from the flames. We won't have anything left to eat if you wait much longer."

Wanda hesitated, but when the liquid began to spill over the top, hissing as it dropped into the fire, she grabbed the wooden spoon from the table. Then, with the use of a towel, she plucked the cauldron from the burning embers and set it aside to cool.

"Thank you. Now, where were we?" Mezzarix asked. "Ah, yes. The Eternity Elixir truly is a remarkable creation. My finest work. Took me two years to complete the mixing process, but once I had, it contained not only the building blocks of life but of death as well. The Eternity Elixir can be combined with any potion to enhance its abilities, it can be substituted for multiple ingredients in any number of potions, and it can reverse and destroy a potion's effects as well. Let's say you wanted to eliminate B.R.E.W. No more laws. No more prisons. A lengthy procedure involving the Eternity Elixir combined with the precious Vessel at B.R.E.W. Headquarters and *poof*." Mezzarix closed his eyes solemnly. "Gone."

"What do you mean *gone*?" Priscilla asked.

"The Vessel would be destroyed and all of its powers reversed. The improvements in science and technology? *Gone*." He grinned. "Plus, no more banishments. No more prisoners. Those who have defied B.R.E.W. would be free to go our merry ways. That's why Esmeralda is interested in the Elixir. Her parents were banished years ago. She probably wants to share some quality time with them before they kick the bucket. That is, if they haven't already done so."

"But someone could just recreate the Vessel, couldn't they?" Priscilla looked to her sister for confirmation.

Mezzarix shook his head vehemently. "Oh, no, my girl. That potion has been bubbling in the chalice for more than three hundred years. No one living knows what is in it or how to reconstruct it. One more thing, my lovely daughters," Mezzarix said. "Should the Eternity Elixir be used to destroy the Vessel and eliminate its powers, all members of the B.R.E.W. Elite would lose their potion making abilities forever."

Priscilla scoffed. "That's a lie!"

Mezzarix looked appalled. "I would never lie to you. You're my flesh and blood. And speaking of blood, that is how it's possible. Wanda made a Blood Link with the Vessel when she became Lead Investigator of B.R.E.W." He tilted his head to the side, eyeing Wanda. "Did you not?"

Wanda opened her mouth, but didn't speak right away. She looked down at the floor. "That's how my judgments are able to hold when I carry them out."

"That Blood Link will be your undoing, should Ms. Faustus succeed with her dastardly plan," Mezzarix said.

Wanda chewed on the inside of her cheek, eyeing her father suspiciously. "It doesn't matter. Even if she did succeed in obtaining the Elixir, she'd never be able to enter B.R.E.W. Without an entry pass, the wards would send her away. And the wards guarding the Vessel are the most powerful ones in existence."

"What if she Blotched an employee with access to the Vessel?" Priss asked.

Wanda shook her head. "Blotching would have no effect against the wards. They would erase the Blotch the moment the individual crossed the barrier. Esmeralda's plan won't work."

Mezzarix chuckled. "My dear, sweet Wanda. You have

grown so much these past twelve years, and yet you're still so naïve. You've never encountered a potion like the Eternity Elixir. The possibilities are endless. Had you both—my own daughters—not stopped me when I did, I would've become the head of B.R.E.W. and enjoyed ultimate power. All because of that clever concoction."

"What are you hinting at?" Wanda asked, leveling her eyes on him.

"Don't you think there's a possibility Esmeralda has considered the wards at the headquarters? It wouldn't take much skill to devise a way past their protections. Not while using the Elixir."

Wanda clenched her jaw. "We need to capture her then."

"And quickly, I suppose. That storm is picking up." Mezzarix pointed to where a wall of white snow obscured visibility beyond the opening of the cave.

Wanda stiffened. "Priss, do you know Esmeralda's whereabouts?"

"She pursued me as far as Europe," Priscilla said. "I couldn't go home. I didn't have time to stop to rest or even call for help. The first moment I had, I mailed the Elixir to you in a secure package, then headed straight for these mountains."

"So she could be anywhere close by."

"No, I don't think so. I haven't seen her for two days. I suspect she may have discovered that I mailed the Elixir and gave up her pursuit. If she knows I sent it to you, that's where she'll be."

Wanda's face paled. She clenched her fists and whirled on her sister. "You've sent that horrible woman to my home? My family! What are my kids supposed to do when she shows up?"

Priss held up her hands. "Relax, Wanda. Your wards are strong, aren't they?"

"Not strong enough for an attack."

"They'll hold," Priss insisted. "Esmeralda is powerful, but without the Elixir in her possession, she won't have an easy way into your home. And I know for a fact your wards are some of the strongest protective spells around. This will all blow over once Esmeralda realizes the Elixir is unattainable."

"Unattainable? But I told you already, I didn't receive any package from you."

"You must have." Priss fumbled in her satchel and pulled out a small ampoule of clear liquid. "I had confirmation that it arrived and was handled by you."

"Then your confirmation potion failed you," Wanda said. "Or someone else handled it by mistake."

"Impossible." Priscilla stared at the ampoule. "I was very specific on who could trigger a confirmation. It had to be my relative, as well as a powerful Elixirist. You're the only one those stipulations could apply to. Well, you and Father, of course."

"Priscilla, listen to me. No package came before I left. So unless . . ." Wanda covered her mouth in shock. "Oh, no! Gordy!"

CHAPTER

14

Gordy leaned over a small pewter cauldron about the size of a cereal bowl. In one hand, he held a slotted spoon. In the other, he clutched the vial of mysterious cream-colored liquid.

"Maybe you should wait until your mom gets back," Adilene suggested.

"She may not be back for a week," Gordy said.

"But you don't even know what it is, or what it does."

"That's why I'm going to attempt to Scrute it. I've seen my mom do this before."

Scruting the contents and properties of an unknown potion required heating the liquid to almost boiling temperatures. Then, while the heat reduced, Gordy would simply add a few drops of quicksilver from his mother's ample supply. The quicksilver enhanced smells and sensations emitted from a potion. In theory, it should be enough for Gordy to Decipher the contents.

"How are you feeling, Max?" Gordy glanced up to check on his friend.

Max slumped in the corner of the lab, the gas mask hanging loosely from his chin. His eyes continually crossed and uncrossed, which was an improvement over how he had been the moment he had unzipped Bawdry's bag. Gordy had never seen anyone faint before. Had it been during different circumstances, he would've shared a laugh with Adilene. But when Max crashed sideways to the floor, he'd nearly pulled Bawdry's mummified body on top of him. Gordy was forced to venture down into the toxic fumes without the aid of the gas mask to help his friend and clean up the mess.

Max blubbered in response, clutching his stomach. "He's so gross! You never said he was that gross!"

"He always said he was that gross," Adilene snapped. "You just never listened."

"Shut up, Rivera." Max's lips clamped together and his cheeks puffed out.

"Don't you dare barf down here," Gordy warned. "I don't have time to clean that up too."

"I'm all right." Max stood and stumbled over to the table.

The fire had heated the pewter cauldron to the proper temperature and, just to be safe, Gordy pointed the oscillating fan so it would blow any noxious vapors away from their workstation.

"Okay, maybe you two should take a step back. I don't

want you to accidentally bump me or anything like that," Gordy said. "I'm just going to put one, maybe two, drops in. That's all. That should be enough."

Gordy uncorked the vial and tilted the opening toward the cauldron. The gooey substance remained clotted at the bottom of the bottle. He swirled it around and tapped the glass with his fingernail. The potion jiggled, then, all at once, the entire mass of liquid slid out and plopped into the cauldron.

"Oh, no!" Gordy shouted.

"That's more than just a drop," Max said.

Gordy frantically tried to ladle the potion out of the cauldron, but the intense heat ignited it instantly. The once-creamy color transformed to dark brown, and the consistency turned from gloppy to crispy in less than a second.

"You're so dead," Max snickered. "Your mom is going to make you give Bawdry a sponge bath."

"Shut up!" Gordy killed the flame to the cauldron. He dashed over to the mini-refrigerator beneath the cupboards and extracted a tray of ice. He dumped the ice cubes into the mess, and they erupted into a hissing cloud of steam that mushroomed up from the opening of the cauldron. When the steam dispersed, Gordy leaned over to look at the damage. All that remained of his aunt's special potion was a streak of black ash.

How could this have happened? He had only intended to add a drop.

"Gordy," Adilene said softly. "It was just an accident. Your mom will understand."

"I should have left it alone. I should have waited."

It wasn't the first time Gordy had ruined a potion. He'd once burned up his mother's entire stock of Komodo dragon saliva in one fell swoop. That had been an expensive mistake. A whole carafe—gone. Punishment was one thing Gordy could handle, but this was different. He didn't know how to explain it to his friends, but he knew in his heart this potion had been special. And just like that, he had destroyed the entire batch. Gordy didn't want to cry, but he could feel hot tears welling up along the rims of his eyelids, threatening to spill over the edges.

Then the doorbell rang upstairs, and Gordy had a feeling that his nightmare of an afternoon was suddenly about to become a lot worse.

Yeltzin stood alone on the porch, stroking his stubbly chin.

"It's the creep from last night," Gordy whispered, stepping back from the peephole in the door. "The one I told you about." He pawed at his eyes and sniffled, but the need to cry had vanished the moment he saw the Russian.

"Where's the lady?" Max asked. "The one with the spiky hair?"

"She's not there," Gordy answered. Yeltzin had parked his white SUV in the center of the driveway.

A sharp rap of knuckles sounded against the door. "Hello, Stitsers. Anybody home? I have question. That is all."

"What do you think he wants?" Adilene asked.

Gordy shrugged. "To find some illegal plant in the living room and shut down my mom's lab, I guess."

"Well, don't open the door," Max said. "Maybe he'll just leave a note or something and go away."

"Good idea," Gordy agreed. "Just stay very—"

"I hear children's voices," Yeltzin interrupted in a sing-song voice. "No need to fear me. I'm not bad guy. I no wish to shut down your mother's lab, whatever that means." He chuckled. "I spoke with your father, and he said is okay. Just open door and I will explain all to you."

Gordy blew out his cheeks. Perfect! Just perfect. He shook his head and reached for the dead bolt.

"What do you think you're doing?" Max asked.

"Keep your voice down!" Gordy hissed. "He knows we're home. He can hear us through the door."

"Yes, Yeltzin has very good ears," Yeltzin said. "Family trait. Like an eagle."

"Eagles have good eyes, not ears," Adilene said, facing the door.

"In Russia, they have both. Come, come. Open door now." He rapped his knuckles once more against the door.

Gordy pulled the chain out of the latch and undid the bolt. "Don't worry. I'm not going to invite him inside," he said.

The door swung in, and Yeltzin's beaming face greeted them warmly. "Hello, young ones. Where is the master of the house?"

Gordy stepped forward. "What do you want?"

"Ah, so *you* are the young master?" Yeltzin gave Gordy a wink. "Listen closely, boy. My employer, Ms. Faustus, has informed me that a package containing substances of an illegal nature and potentially hazardous to good citizens of your neighborhood, may or may not have passed this way within last day or so. Is this true?"

Gordy chewed his bottom lip. "Ah, I don't know. What did it look like?"

"Perhaps this big." Yeltzin held his hands about six inches apart. "And would've come from out of country."

"What was in it?" Max asked.

Yeltzin raised his eyebrow and wiped the corner of his mouth with his thumb. "You have not seen it then?"

All three kids shook their heads.

"You are certain? Because, hear me, boy, if said package did arrive in this home, containing what we think it contained, it would be big blow to your family's well-being. Very unfortunate to mommy and daddy. Perhaps they go away to prison for long time." He planted his fists onto his hips and tapped his boot against the porch.

"Because they received a package?" Gordy scoffed. "They wouldn't go to prison because someone mailed them something."

Yeltzin flipped up his hand and shrugged. "Maybe. Perhaps. We know your mother has not been entirely honest with her practices in this home. We know for fact, she possesses many items that would not be taken lightly by Department of Health and Safety, should they discover. I've seen people go to prison for much less."

Gordy couldn't remember anyone ever complaining about his mom's profession. And now, out of the blue, she was in danger of going to prison? It didn't add up.

Yeltzin didn't add up.

Gordy began to doubt the strangers had anything to do with the Department of Health and Safety. But then who were they really, and what did they want?

"Well, that certainly sounds serious. Thanks for the information." Gordy attempted to close the door, but Yeltzin shot out a meaty hand to stop him.

"It is serious. Now, why don't you let me come inside and take a look around? It would be in your best interest." He took a step through the doorway, but paused. Squinting his eyes, he stared at the ceiling, his nostrils flaring in and out as he inhaled. "What's that burning smell?"

Gordy retreated. "Um . . . uh . . ."

"We burned a batch of brownies," Adilene said.

"That not smell like brownie." Yeltzin took another step and pushed Max out of the way.

Gordy floundered to find his footing as he continued to back away from the door. Yeltzin fixed his eyes on the kitchen, his hands clenching at his sides.

"You can't be here," Gordy stammered. "You have to leave, now!"

As Yeltzin reached forward to push Gordy from his path, the large Russian man made an abrupt stop.

Gordy, Max, and Adilene watched in amazement as Yeltzin's eyes widened and he swiveled on his heels. Then, with his head stiff and rigid, he marched out of the house with lengthy strides. He didn't stop marching until he reached the driver's side door of his SUV and plopped down so heavily in the seat, the axles groaned beneath his weight.

The vehicle's engine roared to life, and the Russian backed down the driveway. Suddenly, he slammed on the brakes, causing his head to bobble back and forth. Yeltzin blinked several times, staring down at the steering wheel in confusion. He dug at his eyes with his fists. Then, with a screech of tires, the SUV sped out of the neighborhood.

Okay, what just happened?" Max demanded, slamming the front door behind him. "One second that man was ready to charge into the kitchen, the next he was tucking his tail between his legs and running out of here."

"That's because of the wards," Gordy explained. "At least now we know they work for sure. But that was close."

"Really close," Adilene agreed. "Gordy, I don't think he's here on behalf of the Department of Health and Safety."

"What are *wards*?" Max asked.

"Protective potions," Gordy said. "My mom sets them up all over the house to keep unwanted people from snooping around. They're activated the moment a member of the family demands that someone leaves the property." He thought back to how scared he had been to tell Yeltzin to leave.

Max stared up at the doorjamb. "That's awesome! Can I get some of those for my house?"

"Um, maybe later." Gordy hurried through the kitchen and down the stairs into the basement. Wasting no time, he tidied up his mess and collected the two now-empty potion vials and returned them to their case. When he resurfaced upstairs, his dad was just entering through the garage door.

"Told you he would be in the lab," Jessica said from behind her dad. "He's always in the there."

Gordy's dad gave him a stern look as he placed the cartons of Chinese food on the kitchen counter. "What were you doing down there?"

Gordy stared at his dad, surprised by how unfriendly he sounded. "Nothing. We were just brewing. And we sprayed Bawdry." Gordy casually slipped the box containing Aunt Priss's vials behind his back.

"You sprayed Bawdry?" His dad crossed his arms and peered over Gordy's shoulder. "What's that smell? It's not Ocean Breeze."

Gordy looked at Max and Adilene for help, but they were too busy trying to sneak their way out of the kitchen.

"No one was here to supervise you," his dad said.

"Supervise me?" Gordy started to smile, but when he realized his dad was serious, his face screwed up in confusion. "Mom lets me go into the lab all the time by myself."

"Then maybe it's time for a change." Mr. Stitser tossed his keys harshly onto the counter. "Something caught on fire. I know that smell, and I'm willing to bet you brewed something you shouldn't have."

Gordy swallowed, squeezing the package tighter in his fingers. Did his dad know the truth?

"You could've burned down the house!" Gordy's dad bellowed.

"No, Dad, it's not like that at all. It was just—"

"Don't you 'Dad' me. Max, Adilene—go home!" Mr. Stitser pointed to the door.

"Yes, sir, Mr. Stitser," Max said, bowing his head respectfully.

"We're sorry if we caused any trouble." Adilene grabbed her jacket from the coat hanger.

"Yeah, try not to kill Gordy, okay? Otherwise, I won't have anyone to copy notes off in geometry." Max grinned, but the smile fell from his face under the force of Mr. Stitser's glare.

"Get out!" Gordy's dad snapped.

Max and Adilene didn't wait around and bolted from the room.

"You didn't have to yell at them. It's not their fault!" Gordy knew his dad had to put his foot down and enforce the rules of the house every so often, but how many times had Gordy gone down into the lab with his dad having full knowledge of it? Loads! And never once had he reacted with such rage.

"No dinner for you tonight. Go to your room and go to bed!"

Was his dad really stressed out from work? Gordy glanced at the microwave clock. "But it's just after five!"

"You're grounded, Gordy. And until you start respecting my rules, you're going to be spending a lot of time in that room of yours."

"Fine!" Gordy stomped away, but stopped at the foot of the stairs. "You should know, Yeltzin came by today and tried to get into the house."

"He did?" Gordy's dad raised his eyebrows thoughtfully. "Did you let him in?"

"No, I didn't let him in! Are you kidding me?"

"You should have. I told him he could come and explore a few of the rooms further." He opened the cupboard and brought out paper plates and plastic cutlery.

"When did you tell him that?" Gordy squeezed the handrail. This was not happening. His mom needed to come home this instant. Clearly, his dad had lost his mind.

"At the grocery store." Mr. Stitser opened the carton of rice and spooned servings onto three paper plates. He then opened a container of sweet and sour chicken. The delicious aroma wafted across the kitchen, and Gordy's stomach grumbled. He had only eaten one *pupusa* at Adilene's. Oh, how he wished he would've ignored his urge to Scrute Aunt Priss's potion.

"I bumped into both him and Ms. Faustus at the store this morning and we had another nice long chat about those allegations," Gordy's dad continued. "I feel it would be in our best interest to not impede their investigation. It will only end up looking poorly on our part. I'll give them a call later this evening and apologize. I trust you weren't rude to Mr. Yeltzin?"

Gordy threw his hands over his head in disgust and stormed up the stairs.

17

The white SUV idled next to a park on the outskirts of the neighborhood. Yeltzin crammed a grease-sopped cheeseburger into his bearded mouth two bites at a time while Esmeralda sat in the passenger seat, eyeing her partner with disgust.

"I think package did arrive." Yeltzin shoved a few French fries into what little space remained in his cheeks, but continued to talk. "Children lie. I read it on their faces."

"Why would they lie?" Esmeralda asked.

Yeltzin wiped his nose with the back of his hand. "Who knows? Kids. They probably just scared, that's all."

"You *are* a tad imposing."

"Me?" Yeltzin swallowed and grinned through his cheeseburger. "I'm a teddy bear."

"And yet you attempted to force your way into their house uninvited." She clucked her tongue. "That was poorly done. You've probably blown our cover, at least with the children."

"Only because I smell strange smoke. But you should know their wards are very strong. I did not have clear head until after driving ten miles to burger restaurant." He looked down at his meal and smacked his lips. "I normally don't enjoy American burgers, but this"—Yeltzin shook the cheeseburger wrapper in his hand—"*this* I like."

"Strange smoke?" Esmeralda checked her makeup in the mirror.

"Strange smoke." Yeltzin nodded. "Potion smoke, but none of which I smelled before. Leads me to believe they may have tested—"

"You don't know what you speak of," she interjected.

"I know what I smelled. Burnt. Coming from basement."

"The boy's a Dram, Yeltzin. From what I'm told, he knows his way around a lab. He could've been brewing any manner of mixtures downstairs."

"Yes, but we both know I don't make many mistakes. I'm a Cipher and a good one at that. I think the boy could've been trying to destroy something he shouldn't. Something he doesn't understand."

Esmeralda narrowed her eyes. "Then we may be running out of time."

"Agreed. Should we launch attack on house?"

Esmeralda blotted her lipstick on one of Yeltzin's unused napkins. "Not yet. If the wards are indeed as strong as you say they are, there could be far greater challenges waiting for us inside. And we don't want to risk anyone alerting the Board before we can prepare. We need solid information. Besides, we know Wanda is away, and my scouts will let me know the instant she lands on American soil."

"Then what do we do?" He swallowed. "Sit here and eat?"

"Absolutely not! I don't have the stomach to watch you gorge yourself on that slop. Tonight, I intend to initiate the next phase of my plan, and we will need to find a place we can hide to scope out their house."

"What? Like spies?"

"If you want to call it that. But we won't be doing the spying." She reached over and dabbed grease from Yeltzin's chin.

CHAPTER

18

Wanda pushed hard against the wind, her boots sinking into thick, wet snow. After an hour of fighting through abysmal weather, she had no idea if she and Priscilla were headed out of the Forbidden Zone or deeper in. The storm had dumped so much snow in so little time.

"I don't think this is the way!" Priscilla caught up with her, breathing hard. "I distinctly remember trees. Don't you remember them?"

Wanda flexed her fingers in her gloves, trying to warm them. "I was too angry with you. I wasn't paying attention."

"Well, I was paying attention, and we would've seen them by now."

"We've been here before, for crying out loud, we should know the way!"

"We were never here during these conditions," Priss said. "We have to stop somewhere to get our bearings."

"Where?" Wanda demanded. "There's nowhere to make shelter, and I can't start a fire out here, exposed!" Her eyes were wet both with the snow and with tears. She spun around, searching, and then saw something. "There! What is that?"

Priss shielded her eyes with her hand and started running. "That's a mountain!"

The two of them raced towards the mountain, unable to see clearly in the maddening flurry of snow. But as they neared it, Wanda suddenly released an angry cry.

Mezzarix stood a few yards outside the entrance of his lair. He wore his cloak wrapped tightly around his head and held a lantern next to his face.

"I thought you two were heading back," Mezzarix called into the wind.

"We got lost," Priscilla explained.

Mezzarix smirked. "Lost? It's just six miles south from here."

Wanda growled in frustration. "How long do you think this storm will last?" she demanded.

Mezzarix stared at the sky and sniffed. "Hard to say. At least another hour or so." He moved next to Wanda, and she felt the warmth from the lantern. "You won't do your family any good dying of hypothermia. Come on. I still have plenty of stew left. You can wait for the storm to pass and then you'll be on your way."

Wanda and Priscilla followed their father back into

the cave. Seated around the table, Wanda eyed her bowl of stew but refused to take a bite.

Priscilla ate ravenously, indulging herself with another helping.

"Tell me about Gordy." Mezzarix slid his bowl to the side and pressed his fingertips together. "He sounds to be a gifted boy. How old is he now?"

"He's twelve," Priss said. "And he's extraordinary."

"Twelve?" Mezzarix gaped at Wanda in shock. "You were pregnant when you carried out my banishment? How did I not know that?"

"Maybe because you were too busy formulating plans for your takeover to be paying attention," Wanda said.

"Maybe. So, Gordy is short for Gordon—named after his father. I've met him?" Mezzarix asked.

"You were at the wedding." Wanda glanced back at her father.

"Ah, that's right. I remember. Gordon didn't have the gift. And the three of you live in that house in Ohio?"

"Five," Priscilla corrected.

"What?" Mezzarix looked shocked.

"There are five of them. Wanda has a set of twins as well."

"Twins. How delightful! A family of brewers."

"The twins don't brew," Wanda said.

"Oh." Mezzarix frowned. "Then let's not talk about them. I want to know more about Gordy. What talents does he possess? Deciphering? Restorative? Philter?"

Wanda raised her eyebrows. "Why do you want to know?"

"Why not? We're not talking about anything else right now, are we?"

"Yes," Priscilla answered. "He has all of those talents. And he can even Blind Batch."

"Be quiet, Priscilla!" Wanda smacked the table. "He doesn't need to know everything. Besides, Gordy is still developing. He has a lot to learn."

Mezzarix interlocked his fingers and rested them on the table. "Blind Batching at such an early age is rare. He doesn't sound to be still developing. Not too many people have that gift. I, of course, am one of them, but it would appear the talent skipped a generation." Mezzarix pouted and pointed at Wanda. "I'm so proud of him, and yet I've never met the child." He stood and sauntered over to the mouth of the cave. "I don't think the storm will stop to-night," he said, searching for a break in the clouds. "And it's getting dark. This will all be ice soon. My recommendation would be to wait until morning."

"I'm going." Wanda zipped up her parka. "You can stay if you'd like, Priss, but I'm not waiting any longer."

Mezzarix tapped his finger on his lip. "There might be another option. A temporary solution to our predicament. It would be tricky to pull off, but if the three of us combine our skills, it just might work."

"What are you talking about?" Wanda asked.

Mezzarix made a sudden sharp whistle, and Wanda

and Priscilla recoiled from the sound. From somewhere down one of the corridors, there arose the *clickity-clack* of footsteps on stone.

———

Wanda and Priscilla stood at the far corner of the cave while their father made the finishing touches on his potion. The golden liquid inside Mezzarix's cauldron produced an effervescent fizz. Doll, the skeleton, stood next to his master, unmoving.

"I don't like this at all," Wanda whispered to her sister. "If we do this, there's a chance we lose all control over the situation."

"Not if all three of us share equally in the potion," Priscilla reasoned. "We've done this before and it worked."

Wanda watched as Mezzarix spooned the potion from the cauldron and dripped the gold liquid over Doll's egg-shaped head. Once Wanda and Priscilla had completed their portions and covered the rest of Doll's head with liquid, the skeleton stiffened, and tiny tremors traveled up his spine.

"Fine work, my dears, this will do lovely. Once Doll has crossed the border of the Forbidden Zone, the Sevite Syrup will bind him to the three of us, so long as we grasp hands. He can be given extensive instructions, that we all agree upon, of course. For example, should we all agree to instruct Doll to protect Gordy—"

"Not just Gordy," Wanda interrupted. "My whole family needs protection."

Mezzarix groaned. "Yes, well, I was merely making an example. But if it makes you feel better, should we all agree to instruct Doll to protect your *family* at all costs, Doll will comply."

"By what means?" Priscilla asked.

Mezzarix raised an eyebrow. "By any means necessary."

"No violence," Wanda said. "I don't want my children witnessing anything like that."

Mezzarix sniffed. "Will Esmeralda offer your family the same 'no violence' guarantee? What do you think, Priss? Is that in her nature?"

Priscilla looked at her sister and then back at Mezzarix. "Doll can do what he needs to in order to protect the Stitsers, but no one is to be seriously injured or killed."

"I think we should also be very explicit on his instructions," Wanda said, crossing her arms. "I don't want your pet interacting with my family if there's not a need. Will he be able to follow that rule?"

"If we all agree to it, there really is no limit to what Doll can do." Mezzarix rested his hand on the skeleton's shoulder bone.

"How can he travel through the blizzard?" Priscilla asked.

"Weather has no effect on him," Mezzarix said. "And he has a perfect sense of direction."

"Then we could follow him off this mountain," Wanda said.

"Oh, no." Mezzarix shook his head. "He would lose you in a matter of seconds. He's far too swift for you to keep up with him. We are running out of time. Are there any other questions?"

"How will Doll get all the way back to my home?" Wanda asked. "There's an ocean in the way, in case you forgot."

"Already thought of that." Mezzarix pointed to Wanda's satchel. "I assume you have your identification, passport, credit cards."

Wanda flinched. "Yes, so—"

"Shush, dear, don't interrupt." Mezzarix nodded at Priscilla. "And you still have your Disfarcar Gel, do you not?"

Priscilla looked down at her bag and scoffed. "You really think we can disguise Doll as Wanda and have it fly all the way from Greenland to Ohio without anyone noticing?"

"Well, that depends," Mezzarix said.

"On what?"

"On how good you are at concocting Disfarcar Gel."

Lying on his bed, Gordy scribbled notes in his potion journal. He had once again hidden the box in his closet, but he wasn't sure why he bothered. Now that both bottles were empty, what was the point of keeping them safe?

Downstairs, Gordy's dad and siblings were watching *Escape from Skull Island*. It was a movie Gordy really wanted to watch, but his dad wasn't budging. No dinner. No television. No freedom. All because his dad suddenly freaked out about Gordy going into the lab, which was something he had done on almost a daily basis.

Gordy's cell phone chirped as a text came through. It was from Max.

Are you dead?

Gordy pressed the lead of his pencil with his thumb and tossed it aside.

Might as well be, he responded.

Never seen ol' Gordon that mad before, Max wrote. *I almost peed my pants.*

Gordy chuckled as he remembered the looks on Max and Adilene's faces when his dad exploded. It wasn't funny at the time, but now it was the only bright spot of the evening.

What are you going to do about the potion?

This text came from another sender—Adilene.

Gordy looked over to where the empty bottles lay beneath his carpet.

Not sure. Not much I can do, I guess.

Could you recreate it somehow? Adilene asked. *Mix some of your mom's ingredients to make another potion just like it?*

I don't know how. I never got a chance to figure out what was in it.

If only he had been more careful. He should've been prepared for the potion's consistency. Not all liquids simply dripped out of their vials. Some plopped, some slinked, some swirled. Gordy's mom had taught him that years ago.

Maybe you could look up what the potion was in one of your mom's books, Adilene suggested. *She probably has something written about it down in the lab. It's worth a shot.*

Adilene had a point. There was no need to give up without at least trying to find a solution to the problem. Then again, Gordy had seen most, if not all, of his mom's creations. Plus, the sheer mystery of Aunt Priss's potion made it seem unlikely he would find a source in one of the many manuals in the lab. Not to mention his dad had grounded him for the rest of his life. If he so much as stepped foot in the lab without permission, Gordy might be given up for adoption.

I'll think of something, Gordy texted back.

He was weird today, don't you think? Max continued with his thread.

What are you talking about? Gordy had forgotten all about Max's conversation.

Your dad. He's not acting like himself.

I know, Gordy typed. *But I feel bad. I lied to him.* He remembered back to the phone conversation with his father and how he'd kept the truth about Aunt Priss's package.

So? I lie to my dad all the time. It's good for him, Max said. *But it's like your dad's possessed.*

Gordy blinked. He didn't know anything about being possessed. That type of thing never happened in the potion community. On the other hand, there was a condition Elixirists commonly referred to as Blotched. It was when someone was unknowingly under the influence of a controlling potion. Gordy thought about his dad's behavior. How he allowed complete strangers into the house without any thought of who they might be. Then there was his sudden eruption of anger. And now his dad was planning on inviting Ms. Faustus and Yeltzin back into their home to investigate. He may not have a clue on how to concoct potions, but Gordy's dad did understand the importance of protecting the family secrets.

Gordy mashed the buttons on his cell phone. *Max, you're a genius!*

This is Adilene, dummy, Adilene responded.

Whatever, Gordy typed. *I'll talk to you both tomorrow.*

He dropped the phone onto his desk and stared at his door. The sounds of swashbuckling pirates rang out from the downstairs television. Gordy could smell buttered popcorn, but he no longer cared. Could his dad really be Blotched? It seemed far-fetched, and yet everything pointed to it being true. There was no doubt Ms. Faustus and Yeltzin were a couple of frauds. But how had they done it? From what he had studied, Blotching only lasted for short periods of time. An hour at most. Gordy's dad had been acting strangely for almost an entire day.

Gordy began pacing the room. Maybe it wasn't a case of Blotching. Maybe it was just stress. Besides, in order for a Blotching to last that long, there would have to be something constantly close enough to contact his dad's body. Like a tainted object. A necklace or a watch or a . . .

Gordy's mouth dropped open as he remembered how Esmeralda Faustus had first introduced herself to his father. It hadn't seemed out of the ordinary at the time, since Gordy hadn't suspected the odd woman and her partner of being enemies to the family. Now there was no mistaking Esmeralda's strange behavior when she'd handed Gordy's dad her business card.

CHAPTER

20

The bottom stair creaked under Gordy's foot, and he cringed. Though the creak wasn't very loud, Gordy couldn't risk getting caught. Not after everything that had happened earlier and with the possibility of his dad being Blotched. He paused before moving onto the hardwood floor and peered over his shoulder to listen. No sounds of movement. The movie had ended two hours earlier, and the whole house had fallen into a calm silence, making every footstep seem like he was falling through the floor.

Crossing through the living room, he made sure not to accidentally bump into any pieces of furniture lurking in the shadows along the way. Once in the kitchen, he looked for his dad's wallet. With the exception of an empty popcorn bag spilling out a few kernels, the countertop was clear. Gordy checked the baker's rack, but found nothing.

"Come on!" he muttered under his breath. "Where is it?" If it wasn't in the kitchen, it could only mean the wallet was in his dad's room. How was he supposed to sneak in there without waking him up?

Suddenly, Gordy heard a soft thump from downstairs in the lab. Cocking his head, he listened, wondering if he had just imagined it.

There it was again! Movement.

Holding his breath, Gordy approached the basement door and pressed his ear against the wood. He heard the sound of footsteps, the crunch of glass, and then one of the drawers of the filing cabinet slid shut. Gordy's heartbeat thudded in his chest. They were being robbed! It had to be that crazy Russian. But how had he gotten past the wards? The ones on the doors and windows were incredibly strong, but they were no comparison to the ones protecting the lab. Gordy had to do something. Wake his father or call the police, maybe.

As he backed away from the door, the sound of heavy footsteps landed on the basement stairs. They rose hastily, and before Gordy could turn to run, the door flew open.

"What are you doing up?" Gordy's dad was still dressed in his blue jeans and a white, collared work shirt, but he was barefoot and holding a dustpan.

"Uh . . . um . . ." Gordy was so relieved not to see Yeltzin standing before him that he had lost all ability to speak.

His dad scowled. "You should be in bed."

"I didn't get anything to eat for dinner and I was starving." That wasn't entirely a lie. Gordy was hungry.

The scowl softened. "Of course you are. I should've brought you something earlier. There's leftover Chinese food in the fridge. Noodles and rice, and I think there may be some orange chicken in one of the boxes. I can heat some up for you in the microwave," his dad offered.

"What were you doing down there?" Gordy asked.

Mr. Stitser glanced down at the dustpan and puffed out his cheeks. "We have a problem, son." He turned toward the door leading downstairs.

The lab was trashed. Bottles lay overturned on the apothecary tables. Broken glass littered the floor, and every filing cabinet drawer had been pulled out and emptied, the papers scattered throughout the room. Two vials of potions had been dumped. Steam rose from one of them, while the other bubbled. The smell was horrific, but it wasn't coming from the spilled potions. Whoever had snuck into the lab had opened Bawdry's covering. The smell alone should've incapacitated the intruder.

Shielding his mouth and nose with his sleeve, Gordy doused Bawdry with a heavy dose of air freshener before carefully zipping back up his bag.

"What happened down here?" Gordy had never seen the lab in such disarray.

"I was hoping you would have the answer," his dad replied. "But first, are we in danger of inhaling any sort of poison or chemical from those?" He pointed to the puddles of multicolored goop.

Gordy uncovered his nose and took a deep breath.

He didn't think the potions were dangerous, but he knew how to be sure. Inhaling through his nostrils, he caught a whiff of chokecherry pits, millipede antennae, armadillo spleen, and just a hint of rosewood. That was one of his mother's fireless heating potions. She often brought it along on camping trips.

Gordy tested the second. He sensed granulated turquoise, bladderpods, yellow trumpet vine, and a hearty portion of Japanese eggplant. Though it was more exotic than the other one, that potion was used for deep-sea divers to give them the freedom of diving and rising out of the ocean with no need of decompressing. It was an expensive potion though, because bladderpods were difficult to harvest. Gordy's mom was going to be ticked!

"We're safe," Gordy said.

"Good. Now, start explaining yourself." His dad fixed him with a withering stare.

"You think I did this?"

"Not necessarily. Maybe you're covering for your friends, Max and Adilene."

"When would they have wrecked the lab? You saw us earlier when you came home, and it wasn't messed up then."

"I didn't go down into the lab at first. It was only a little while ago I decided to check it out. Gordy, this is serious. I've never known you to do something so irresponsible."

"It wasn't me!"

"Who, then? Isaac or Jessica? They wouldn't know how to work the combination, which means *you* were careless and left it unlocked. Still your fault."

"I—" Gordy shook his head. "No, I don't think it was them. They know better." It would have been easy to blame this on his younger brother and sister. They were rambunctious and messy, but this was well beyond their area of expertise.

His dad swept a pile of a powdery substance into the dustpan. "Which leaves only you, Gordy. Were you trying to cover this up? Is that why you came downstairs tonight? You thought I was asleep and had the perfect opportunity to sneak in here and clean everything before I was any wiser?"

"I would never do this. Just listen to me, please! I think Yeltzin did this. When he showed up earlier, he was really pushy. He tried to get into the house without permission, but Mom's wards turned him away."

"Oh, give it a rest, Gordon. You can't always pass blame to someone else. And now there's a huge mess to clean up. This is your fault, and lying about it is only going to make things worse for you!"

Gordon? His dad never called him Gordon. He used any number of nicknames—Gordy, Gordo, Gordster, Gordelicious—but never Gordon. Gordy's mom called him Gordon when she was really upset, but then it was always accompanied by his middle name, Ethan, and junior at the end.

His dad spun around and emptied the dustpan into a trashcan.

And that's when Gordy saw it.

The square shape of his dad's wallet bulging in his back pocket.

Then it all made sense.

Gordy's dad had been Blotched and was now being controlled by Esmeralda and Yeltzin to search for something in the lab. Gordy was willing to bet his potion journal that they were hunting for Priscilla's mysterious potions. That's why the wards didn't work. They weren't designed to prevent a family member from wandering in and out of the lab.

Gordy's dad shoved the contents of the filing cabinet back into the drawers and brushed broken glass off the apothecary table into the trashcan. "There's no excuse for this. No excuse!" he growled.

Eyes darting around the room, Gordy saw several of his mom's potions still intact on the tables. He could tell what they contained by their color and consistency. He noticed a bottle of Heliudrops, perfect for kite flying, two flasks of Anti-Loitering Lotion that his mom used at the end of her neighborhood skin cream parties, and several beakers of Boiler's Balm, which worked far better than any bandage known to man. All of those were great concoctions, but none of them solved his predicament. Then Gordy spotted a thin vial of Torpor Tonic. The contents of that bottle would knock anyone unconscious for a short period of time.

Gordy's dad was no longer acting on his own, and he posed a serious threat to the family's safety. Gordy didn't want to knock him out, but it was the only choice he had.

"You're right," Gordy said with a sigh. "I did this."

"What?" His dad whirled around. "You did?"

"Yeah." Gordy stared at the floor. "I was trying to show off to my friends, and I slipped."

His dad nodded. "And you knocked everything over and didn't have time to clean it up."

"Exactly. I'm worthless." Gordy considered whipping up some tears to help with the convincing, but they weren't necessary.

His dad shook his head in disappointment. "You may be grounded for a long time. Do you know that?"

"Here, let me help clean up." Gordy stepped over piles of glass and dirt, winding his way over to the table. He straightened a few parchments of potion ingredients and ran his hand down the row of glass containers until finally resting upon the one he needed. Uncorking the vial, Gordy pressed his thumb over the opening. He shook it, agitating the liquid into a swirling froth of emerald-colored bubbles.

Did he really have to do this? He was already in a world of trouble for taking the blame for the mess, but what if his dad really wasn't Blotched? Could Gordy risk using a semi-dangerous potion on one of his parents?

He felt his father's hand on his shoulder. "You know,

son, I don't think I need your help. I want you out of here. In fact, you're not going to stay here until your mother gets back to sort this out. Go pack your things. You'll sleep at Grandma and Grandpa Stitsers for the rest of the week."

It was such a ridiculous punishment, which merely solidified what Gordy believed to be true.

"I'm sorry, Dad," Gordy whispered.

"Sorry doesn't cut it, Gordon," his dad answered. "Not this time."

"No." Gordy turned around. "I'm sorry for this." He removed his thumb, and a thin column of bubbles shot out of the vial and into his dad's face.

Gordy's dad collapsed to his knees, his chin drooping to his chest and a trickle of drool falling from his open mouth.

"Seriously, Dad, I am so sorry!" Gordy left his dad on the ground as he rushed over to the table and scrounged around for a pair of rubber gloves, which he pulled on immediately. "And I'm so dead if you wake up before I figure this out."

Most Torpor Tonics could be clocked to last exactly ten minutes if brewed by a skilled Elixirist using an Amber Wick. Gordy's mom was more than skilled, so he trusted it. After grabbing a pouch of pink detection powder and placing a Bunsen burner under a small stone cauldron, Gordy returned to his dad. He gently pushed him forward and fished out the wallet from his dad's jeans.

The detection powder crackled as it came in contact with Esmeralda's business card.

"I knew it!" Gordy pumped his fist. He checked the

clock above the fireplace and noted he had eight minutes remaining until the Torpor Tonic wore off. "Now to destroy this puppy."

Gordy tested the temperature in the cauldron. He turned down the lights in the room and poured in several drops of liquefied wormwood, a plastic thimble of powdered buckeyes, and a teaspoon of charcoal shavings from an artist's pencil. All at once, the mixture became a solid substance, similar in texture to Silly Putty. With a pair of tongs, Gordy placed the business card in the cauldron and stood back. The card produced a high-pitched whine and then disintegrated just as the Torpor Tonic's effects ended.

Gordy's dad woke up. "What happened?" His dad stared blankly around the room, his eyes struggling to focus. "It's like I . . . fell or something. Did I fall?" Dazed, he looked up at Gordy and smacked his lips. "I think I must have fallen down the stairs."

"No, Dad, you didn't fall," Gordy said.

"Maybe I need to install an elevator or someth . . . Wait a minute . . . I remember something." He looked around the room again, but this time his eyes were focused. "I was going to buy Chinese food for dinner. Orange chicken. Shrimp wontons. But it's past dinner, isn't it? What time is it? Did you make this mess?"

"Dad, listen to me." Gordy knelt next to his father, staring intently into his eyes. "I didn't make the mess."

"Oh, good, Gordo. It's not like you to destroy things. So who tore up your mom's lab?"

Gordy exhaled. "You did."

"Me?" Gordy's dad dug at the corners of his eyes with his fists. "What's going on? I don't feel right."

Gordy patted his dad on the shoulder and explained everything that had happened to him over the past two days.

Wanda patiently inched her way down the aisle of the airplane as the other passengers stored their bags in the overhead compartments. Most of the passengers were native to Greenland, but a few spoke English.

A balding flight attendant reached down and clasped the handles of Wanda's satchel. "Can I stow that for you, miss?" he asked with a cheesy grin.

Wanda jerked the satchel away and raised it up, hugging it to her chest.

"Oh, I do apologize. I was simply trying to help."

Wanda ignored him. When a path cleared down the aisle, she continued walking until she found her seat next to the window at the rear of the plane.

She buckled the seat belt in her lap and tucked her satchel down by her feet.

A heavyset man with a laptop crowded in next to her.

"Mind if I have the window?" the man asked. "I like to watch the water."

Wanda glanced at the window and slid the blinder shut. She then tightened the strap of her seat belt.

The heavyset man harrumphed and went about logging onto his laptop.

"I'm sorry, sir," a female flight attendant apologized. "You'll have to stow that until after the captain gives the all clear."

The passenger and flight attendant argued for a moment as the pilot's voice echoed through the airplane.

Expressionless, Wanda stared at the back of the seat in front of her and paid no attention to the bits of information the pilot shared over the intercom.

"Ma'am? Excuse me, ma'am." The flight attendant raised her voice from the aisle.

Wanda turned her head and looked at the woman.

"Can I get you a pillow or a blanket?" the flight attendant asked.

Wanda tilted her head to the side, regarding the woman as though she were nothing more than an enormous pile of bat guano that happened to have the power of speech.

Wanda shook her head and returned to staring at the seat in front of her.

~

Meanwhile, the real Wanda paced back and forth inside Mezzarix's cave while a horrendous blizzard howled and dumped buckets of snow all along the slopes of Mount Forel.

Wanda couldn't relax. She was nervous. There were too many ways for their plan to fail. What if the flights were delayed? What if someone noticed something peculiar about the passenger onboard the airplane and notified security? Priscilla's perfectly crafted Disfarcar Gel would last precisely twenty-four hours. That seemed like a sufficient amount of time at first, but the air travel from Nuuk, Greenland, to Dayton, Ohio, would take close to nineteen hours. Add in the time it would take Doll to travel from the cave to the nearest airport and pass through customs, and there was no telling where the impostor Wanda could be when the gel wore off, revealing a frightening skeleton with an egg-shaped stone head and holding a burlap sack containing Wanda's personal belongings in its lap.

CHAPTER

23

Two days later, Gordy sat in the cafeteria next to Max and Adilene. He had just finished telling them about the previous night's incident in the lab. There were other kids seated at the long table, but they weren't paying attention so Gordy spoke freely in between bites of his corn dog.

"What happened after you destroyed the business card?" Max asked.

"You have mustard all over your face," Adilene said, pointing at the gobs of yellow sauce painting the corners of Max's mouth.

Max jabbed his tongue out and licked. "Thanks, Rivera." He failed at removing even a portion of the mustard from his lips.

"My dad completely snapped out of it," Gordy said. "Destroying that business card made him go back to normal."

"He wasn't mad about the mess?" Adilene chewed on one of the carrot sticks from her lunch.

"Not at all. I'm not even grounded anymore. My dad felt so bad about how he treated me that he said he was going to rent another movie for me to watch tonight if I want to, even though it's a school night. He also said it was all his fault."

"It *was* all his fault," Max agreed, sneaking a fry from Gordy's lunch tray.

"Not really. It could have happened to anyone who answered the door. That Esmeralda lady was fast, and she knew how to talk and confuse you." Gordy took a sip of chocolate milk. "Anyways, we spent another hour cleaning everything up, and then I went to bed."

"What's going to happen now?" Adilene asked.

"Yeah, what are you going to do when those two come knocking at the door again?" Max added. "I bet you anything they will."

"Well, I'm not going to open it."

"Are you sure they really want your aunt's potion?" Adilene removed a carton of hummus and some celery sticks from her lunch sack. "It seems like a lot of trouble for something so small."

"Uck." Max gagged. "What is that gunk?"

"This is hummus. It's healthy and delicious," she said.

"It looks like one of Gordy's barfing potions."

"They have to be after Aunt Priss's potion," Gordy

said. "Remember what Yeltzin was asking about? A package from out of the country. That's what they want."

"You should call the Feds," Max said. "They could surround the house with guns and wear bulletproof vests and arrest Yeltzin and that Esmeralda chick." Gordy started laughing, and Max frowned. "What? I'm being serious. You don't know what these guys are capable of."

"How are the police going to stop them?" Adilene asked. "They don't know what to do with potions. And wouldn't that break one of the five main rules of potion making? Something about drawing unnecessary attention to the world of wonder?"

Gordy nodded. "She's right. We'd have to wipe their memories completely after their investigation. And that can be tricky and dangerous."

Max glared at Adilene. "Fine. Then the next time Esmerelda and Yeltzin show up, you call me, Gordy. I'll come over and—"

"You?" Adilene laughed. "What could *you* possibly do to them?"

"Guys, stop arguing," Gordy said. "Let's just hope they stay away until my mom gets back."

"At least you stopped your dad before he did any real damage to the house." Adilene lowered her voice as a couple of their classmates walked past their table with lunch trays in hand.

"Yeah." Max leaned in. "Can you imagine what he must've looked like when he was tearing up the place? I bet you he was like a zombie with his eyes rolled in the back of his head and his mouth all . . ." He opened his mouth, and his tongue dangled out.

Gordy grinned. "I don't even want to think about that. I'm just glad I don't have to worry about him anymore."

～⌒

Disaster had struck the Stitser house when Gordy returned home from school. Springs and fluff poked out from the couch. Gordy's dad's recliner lay upside down, the arms broken, the pillows turned inside out. The kitchen was in a similar state. Most of the refrigerator's contents lay scattered across the floor: eggs, ketchup, and Chinese leftovers. Some sort of disgusting slime trailed its way from the kitchen into the living room. It probably came from one of the overturned bottles of barbecue sauce, but Gordy wasn't sure. Every cabinet and drawer in the kitchen had been emptied.

"What is going on?" Gordy ran his fingers through his hair. First it was the lab and now this.

As Gordy began cleaning up the mess, his thoughts turned to his bedroom, and more importantly, his secret hiding place. Bounding up the stairs, Gordy raced through the hall and breathed a deep sigh of relief when he found his room had been untouched. In fact, nothing beyond the living room had been ransacked. It was as if the intruders had caught a whiff of Gordy coming home and had high-tailed it out of there. Other than Gordy, there was no one else in the house, not even in the basement lab, which had been trashed once again.

Gordy replaced the cushions in the wingback chairs and sat down, opening one of his mom's potion manuals in his lap. She always kept this copy in her top dresser drawer for emergencies. It was the "Family Use" potion manual, but only Gordy knew how to use it. The television played in the background, but Gordy had more important things to do than watch. Flipping to the middle of the book, he found the heading he was looking for.

TESTING THE HOME WARDS

He had never tested the wards before, nor had he seen his mom do it, but it couldn't be that complicated. One of the wards must have been broken or faulty. It was the only explanation for the disaster. Well, not the *only* explanation, but Gordy wasn't ready to pass blame to his dad again just yet. Burning the business card should've handled the situation, unless Esmeralda and Yeltzin had taken extra measures to keep Gordy's dad Blotched.

His mom had drawn a detailed diagram pinpointing the location of each of the wards. To Gordy's surprise, there were actually more than forty protecting the house. They were above doorways, below windowsills, around toilets, heater vents, the attic door. Basically any opening from the outside required protection. Gordy figured there would be multiple wards guarding the lab, but he was surprised at how many had been placed on the garage. There were several along the fence and even a couple on the mailbox. One of them was located at the top of the buckeye tree that had branches spilling over into the neighbor's yard.

"How could anyone know where all of them are?" Gordy muttered in amazement. His mom had always been cautious, but this was absurd.

Just then someone knocked sharply on the door. Before Gordy could answer it, the door swung open and Max and Adilene bounded in. Panicked, Gordy had texted them the moment he had discovered the mess, and they immediately rushed over.

"Who did this, Gordy?" Adilene asked as she picked up a few magazines from the carpet.

"I don't know."

"Are they still here?" Max asked, eyes wide.

Gordy shook his head. "No one was here when I got home."

"How can you know for sure?" Adilene sat down next to Gordy on the couch.

"I checked every room in the house when I looked for all the damage. No one's here." He hoped the wards were still working.

"It has to be your dad, dude," Max said. "He must still be Blotched."

The garage door rumbled open as the family van pulled inside. Gordy's dad entered the house along with the twins he had picked up from school. Upon entering the room, Mr. Stitser gaped openmouthed at the damage, and then shared an awkward silent moment with Gordy.

"It happened again." Gordy's voice cracked. He didn't know why, but he felt on the verge of crying. Maybe it was because he was struggling to keep control of the house while his mother was away.

"You're busted, Mr. Stitser!" Max cheered, unable to control his excitement. "Now the question is, did you find what you were looking for?"

Mr. Stitser scratched the back of his head. "You think I did this? Guys, I've been at work all day."

Isaac and Jessica kept a safe distance from the destruction. They usually enjoyed good healthy clutter and would happily make a mess whenever possible. But now they stood by the garage door, staring with their mouths open at the scene as though it were a pool of acid.

"How do we know you really went to work?" Max asked.

"Max!" Adilene snapped. "You don't have a brain, do you?"

"I'm just saying." Max folded his arms. "We have witnesses. All three of us can prove where we were, but who's gonna vouch for him?" He nodded at Mr. Stitser.

Gordy held up his mom's manual. "I don't know if Dad did this or not. I need to test the wards first."

Everyone crowded into the Stitser lab while Gordy grabbed a stainless steel cauldron to create the testing potion. Normally, it would have taken him just a few minutes to accomplish, had the lab not been in yet another state of disorder. Whoever had been there, whether it was his dad or someone else, they were being bold with their search. Ransacking the house in the middle of the day showed how desperate they had become. The next stop would be the upstairs and then—game over.

Gordy completed the potion and grabbed a pair of thick, yellow dish gloves. He fitted a pair of goggles over his eyes and then carefully transferred the contents of the cauldron to a plastic spray bottle. The clear container turned bright pink.

"Stay back, and don't let any of the potion touch your skin," Gordy warned.

"What happens if it touches your skin?" his dad asked, sliding in front of the twins.

"Not sure. But it probably won't feel too good," Gordy explained. "This is liquefied detection powder. By spraying it on or around the wards, it should let us know if they're still working without damaging the ward. If the ward has been broken, nothing will happen."

"And if the ward is still working?" Adilene asked.

Gordy glanced down at the manual, his lips moving silently as he read. "It will hiss like a snake."

"Wicked!" Max rubbed his hands together.

Gordy pointed the spray bottle next to the doorway leading into the lab and pulled the trigger. An immediate, sharp-sounding hiss erupted from the wood. He made his way over to the fireplace. He sprayed the potion and heard a similar hiss. He grew frustrated. Part of him wanted the wards to be broken. Not only would it explain how some-one got into the house but it would also prove his dad's innocence. But as he tested each and every ward—in the yard, around the garage, inside the mailbox, atop the buck-eye tree—and found that all of them were still intact, he didn't know what to do.

"What does this mean?" his dad asked.

"Isn't it obvious?" Max said. "They still have you voo-doo'ed."

"How though?" His dad pulled his wallet from his back pocket. He removed his credit cards and a few dollar bills. "There's nothing in here that could be from them, and I haven't seen Esmeralda since that first evening."

"You told me you met her and Yeltzin at the grocery store the other day. Do you remember that?" Gordy asked.

"I did?"

"Yes," Gordy said. "You said you told them it would be okay if they came by the house."

Max snapped his fingers. "They must've zapped you then."

"I said that?" Gordy's dad looked stunned. He closed his eyes and shook his head. "I don't remember ever going to the grocery."

Gordy looked away from his dad. "The wards wouldn't affect you like they would a stranger or an intruder. You can go anywhere you want throughout the house. You can tear everything up and nothing will happen."

"But you destroyed the business card," Gordy's dad

said. "That was supposed to do something, right? Like snap me out of my trance. How could it still be happening? And what about Max and Adilene?" He glanced at Gordy's friends. "How are they able to come and go whenever they please? Did your mother make an exception for them?"

"No, but I did. They have my permission to enter the house whenever they want. That's how the wards work. Anyone can come over as long as they're invited, but they have to leave the moment someone who lives here wants them to."

His dad sighed. "Then the same condition applies to the three of you. I'm not saying I'm not at fault here, but we can't necessarily rule out the possibility that Max and Adilene, or even you, Gordy, are guilty of tearing up the house."

"I agree with Gordy's dad. How would we know if we were Blotched or not?" Adilene looked at Gordy for the answer.

"I don't know. We'd have to find out if there were items on us that had been tampered with. And we'd probably need to test everything."

"You're not spraying me with that pink Kool-Aid," Max said. "Besides, I think I have a better idea."

"Oh, really?" Adilene mocked.

"A stakeout!"

Adilene groaned. "Why do you always bring it back to food? I'm a vegetarian; I don't eat steak."

"Not that kind of steak." Max fixed Adilene with a

withering look. "A stakeout. Like when cops go undercover and hide out to catch criminals in the act. We could spend the night and set up checkpoints and shifts. It would be awesome!"

"That's not a bad idea," Gordy said.

Adilene's eyes grew large. "I can't sleep over. It's a school night, and you guys are boys! My parents would never let me do that."

"That's too bad, Rivera." Max scrunched his lips. "We'll have to tell you how it goes. You know that my parents don't care if I stay," he said to Gordy. "They love it when I'm not home. Gives them some peace and quiet."

"Can we stay up too?" Isaac asked his dad. "And could you make popcorn?"

"Absolutely not!" Gordy's dad protested. "Adilene's right. It *is* a school night, and I have work in the morning. I won't allow it."

"Ah." Max nodded slowly. "That makes sense."

"It does?" Gordy looked at Max, bewildered.

"Yeah. Mr. Stitser is afraid we'll blow his whole operation, aren't you?"

"What? No!" Gordy's dad shouted.

"Don't get mad. I'm just saying what everyone else is thinking."

"You're the only one thinking that, Max." Mr. Stitser looked at Gordy. "Right?"

Gordy shuffled his feet. "Uh . . . well . . . I think Max may be right."

"Oh, dear," Gordy's dad said. "I was afraid you might say that. All right, I'll call my folks. Isaac and Jessica, you two will sleep over at Grandma and Grandpa Stitsers. Sound fun?"

"No!" Isaac pouted. "I want to be here for the stakeout."

"Yeah!" Jessica said, stamping her foot. "Me too!"

Gordy's dad shook his head. "That's out of the question. I'm afraid we'll have our hands full enough as it is with Max staying the night."

CHAPTER

24

W alkie-talkies?"

"Check." The walkie-talkie chirped as Max pressed down the call button. "You there, Rivera?"

There was an eruption of static, but then Adilene responded. "I'm here." Her voice was soft, not much louder than a whisper. "Sorry I can't be there, Gordy."

"It's okay," Gordy said. "You don't have to apologize."

"Still. I wish I could help in some way."

"Just stay on the walkie, and we'll keep you posted of what's going on," Gordy said.

"Deal. Just don't use these radios until after my parents go to bed," she instructed. "Not a minute before ten thirty, okay?"

Max stuck his tongue out at the radio, but turned the volume down.

"Flashlights?" Gordy continued with his checklist.

"Check." Max clicked one of the flashlights on and off and then stuffed it into his backpack.

"Snacks?"

Max glanced over at an empty bag of trail mix. "Yeah, we're gonna need to stock up again."

"You ate that whole bag?" Gordy gaped at Max. "Already?"

"It was low-fat."

"Fine. We'll make a detour to the kitchen before going downstairs. Torpor Tonic?"

"Check . . . I guess." Max held up a vial of green liquid.

"Yeah, that's it. How many do we have?" Gordy hoped they wouldn't be forced to use the knockout potion again, but he wasn't taking any chances.

"Four. Two for each of us. For smashing in your dad's face!"

"Give me those, please." Gordy held out his hand. "You're not smashing anything in my dad's face."

Max reluctantly passed over the vials of Torpor Tonic. "I was just kidding."

"Detection Spray?" Gordy picked up the bottle of pink fluid resting next to him on the bed. "Check. Okay, I think we're set."

Downstairs, Mr. Stitser had been tied up with rope to a folding chair. The rope had been his dad's idea. After all that had happened, Mr. Stitser couldn't be one hundred percent positive that he wasn't the one responsible, and being tied up seemed like the easiest way to keep him out of trouble.

"Are you sure you want to do this?" Gordy had set up

a camera on a tripod in the corner of the room pointing towards his dad's chair.

His dad smiled. "Absolutely! It will be an adventure. I just don't want any of the video showing up on the Internet, agreed?" He scowled at Max. "Could I have a drink of water, Mr. Warden?"

"Quiet, maggot!" Max shouted in his tough-guy voice. "You'll drink when I say you drink! Just kidding, here you go." Max brought a glass of ice water up to Mr. Stitser's mouth and allowed him to sip.

"We'll take two-hour shifts." Gordy checked the time on the DVD player. "Do you want to start in the lab?"

"Nu-uh. No way!" Max protested. "I'm not volunteering to hang out in that freak show. I'm not crazy."

"Is that okay if I go down first?" Gordy asked his dad.

Mr. Stitser glanced at Max and then back at Gordy. "You're going to leave me all alone with him?" But he was smiling. "No, that's fine. Whatever you need to do. We'll be okay."

~

The walkie-talkie squawked, and Gordy waited for a voice to speak through the receiver.

"You still awake?" Adilene asked.

It was eleven thirty, and Gordy had been watching the fireplace for almost two hours straight. So far so good. Not a peep from anyone outside.

"I think so," he said. "I'm tired though. It's hard to keep my eyes open."

"Well, don't close them. If you do that, we won't know for sure who has been destroying the house."

"I know. I'm going to stay awake. I promise." But it was easier said than done. Gordy had brought down his potion journal to occupy his time, and though he had scribbled a few ideas, writing by flashlight was making his head hurt.

"Do you really think your dad's the one trashing your house?" Adilene asked.

Gordy paused before answering. He nervously clicked the eraser end of his mechanical pencil. "No one else can get around as easy. You remember what happened when Yeltzin tried to bully his way in. The wards kicked him out, and they're all still intact—as far as I can tell. Unless they find a way to destroy the wards, no one can come in that doesn't already have permission. And I know it's not me or Isaac and Jessica."

"But you don't know for sure."

"I'm not acting any different, am I?" he asked. "When my dad was Blotched, he got angry really quick and said weird things."

"He's not doing that now, though," she said softly. "Is he?"

"I guess not. But maybe Esmerelda found a way to make him act more normal." That didn't seem likely either.

"I kind of hope it is him, don't you?"

"What?"

"Don't take that wrong, Gordy. Your dad's awesome. He's like the coolest dad ever, but if he's the one trashing the house, it means we don't have to worry about anyone else getting past the barriers.

Gordy sighed. "Yeah, I guess you're right, though I feel awful about it." He shook his head. "This is all my fault."

"How's it your fault?" Adilene asked.

"If I hadn't messed around with that potion . . ."

"Esmeralda and Yeltzin would've still shown up," Adilene said. "It wouldn't have stopped them from coming to your house, or Blotching your dad."

Gordy fell quiet, listening.

"Besides," she continued, "if you hadn't opened your aunt's package, you wouldn't have known how serious it was. Those creeps would've walked right in and taken the potion, and then what? You did the right thing, I think. And your mom will see it that way."

"Thanks, Adilene," Gordy said.

"You're welcome," she replied. "How's your dad doing?"

"He's asleep. So is Max, I think."

More static poured from the walkie-talkie and then Max's voice said, "No, I'm not. But I'm coming down there with you. Your dad snores."

Adilene signed off on the walkie for the night and two minutes later, Max sat cross-legged next to Gordy on the stone floor of the basement.

"What snacks do you have?" Max asked.

Gordy looked into his backpack. "None."

"None? Are you serious?" Max whined.

"You had all the snacks! I didn't bring any downstairs. What do you have left, Max?" Gordy snapped.

Max held up his hands in surrender. "Chill out, all right?"

Gordy stood up and started gathering his things.

"Hey, where are you going?"

"We're swapping shifts," Gordy said. "We can't leave my dad upstairs without anyone watching him."

"We're recording him, and he's sound asleep. The moment he wakes up and starts to go nuts, we'll know." Max stretched his legs and leaned against the wall. "Sit down, please."

Gordy looked at the stairs and chewed on the inside of his cheek. Max had a point. The house was fairly quiet. Any disruption from his dad and they would be the first to know. He sat back down and both of them stared at the fireplace. Outside a strong wind blew, and it howled in the chimney.

"This is worthless," Max groaned. "Your house is so boring at night."

"It was your idea to do this, remember?"

"I thought there would be action, and we would get to throw potions and stuff. I had to sit through an hour of some television show where they took apart ovens and put them back together again. Your dad laughed the whole time like he was watching Saturday morning cartoons."

Max rummaged around in his backpack. He pulled out a candy bar and two cans of soda.

"I thought you said you were all out of snacks."

"Almost. We're down to the last of our rations, sir," Max whispered.

Gordy smirked. "You can't take this serious, can you?"

"I am serious." Max popped open one of the cans and slurped grape soda. "Once this Snickers is gone, we're going to have to start eating each other." He opened his mouth wide, leaned over, and pretended to bite Gordy.

"Get off me!" Gordy laughed. "Quit fooling around."

Suddenly, Gordy stopped. It had been soft and almost unnoticeable, but he swore he had heard something move. "Did you hear that?" he whispered.

Max was guzzling his drink. "Hear what?" He released a deafening belch. "That?" He smiled, and even in the near-darkness of the lab, Gordy could see purple soda staining his teeth.

Gordy clicked on his flashlight. "I thought I heard something. Like someone moving." Straining to listen, he pointed the flashlight up the stairs, and the beam lit up the half-opened door leading into the kitchen. Dust particles swirled in the light like tiny insects. Was this the moment when his dad woke up and started ransacking the place?

"You're just freaked out, that's all. I didn't hear any—" Max stopped talking, and his eyes grew large.

Something was indeed moving, but it wasn't coming from upstairs.

Gordy felt his pulse quicken as he pointed the flashlight back into the lab. He and Max squeezed close to each other as they looked at the fireplace and then at the tables, their flashlights slowly panning from one end of the room to the other. They scanned the floor and then the counters and the numerous vials and flasks, searching for whatever could be making a noise. Maybe it was a lizard or some critter in his mom's cabinets. She did harbor live mice from time to time.

Then Gordy and Max heard the distinct sound of a zipper unzipping, and their flashlight beams fell upon Bawdry's body bag just as a dark, slimy hand poked through the opening.

Thin, rotting fingers flexed, working their way out of the bag. The material bulged and writhed as the opening widened and the zipper inched down to the end. Another hand appeared. It glowed in the two, trembling flashlight beams as Bawdry's awful stench filled the room.

Max swallowed. "Um . . . Gordy, what the—"

Gordy clamped his hand over Max's mouth. "Turn off your flashlight," he whispered. "And don't make a sound."

Max nervously fumbled, but he managed to shut it off just as the decomposing mummy leaned forward and poked his head out of the bag. Oozing bandages covered Bawdry's skin with the exception of his mouth and one of his eyes. His gnarled lips were pulled back in a wide, permanent smile, and his teeth opened and closed, producing a hollow chomping sound.

Bawdry pulled the tubes out of his chest and back and tossed them aside. One of the machines that collected the fluids from the mummy made a soft beep. Hissing, Bawdry reached over and shut off the alarm with his bony finger before the machine could make another chirp.

How was this happening? Bawdry had been dead for at least a thousand years and had been in the Stitsers' lab peacefully up until this moment. Had he been waiting all this time? Did the previous owners, the ones who sold him to Gordy's mom, know of Bawdry's ability? Mummies simply didn't wake back up for no good reason!

One heavily bandaged leg appeared from the bag, and then the other. Bawdry leaned forward, steadied his feet against the floor, and stood up. Gooey, brown flesh poked out from between the wrappings. Bawdry's chest expanded, and he opened his mouth to take in a deep, shuddering breath.

Max whimpered next to Gordy. "I want to go home"

Gordy promptly elbowed him the ribs. "Be quiet!"

"There's a mummy walking around in your basement!" Max pinched his nose. "And he stinks so bad!"

Gordy steadied himself, staring down the monster with his jaw clenched in determination. "Bawdry," he said, his voice clear and unwavering. "Leave now!"

Bawdry cocked his head to the side, listening, his uncovered eye searching the room until he found Gordy. Then he released a low growl, his arms tensing, as something clear and thick dripped from his lips like drool.

"He has to leave, doesn't he?" Max asked. "Won't the wards make him go?"

But nothing happened. Bawdry showed no sign of being coerced by the home wards.

"I'm guessing it's because Bawdry is technically part of our family, or maybe it doesn't work on dead things," Gordy said.

"Yeah, well, he doesn't look dead anymore!"

Gordy reached into his backpack and pulled out two vials of Torpor Tonic. Would they work the same on the dead as they did on the living?

There was a crash from upstairs, and Gordy's dad groaned. "What's going on? Untie me!"

"Untie yourself, Mr. Stitser! We've got bigger problems on our hands." Max reached for one of the vials of Torpor Tonic, and before Gordy could stop him, he hurled the bottle at Bawdry. The shot sailed wide, missing the mummy by at least a foot, and shattered against the wall. Green steam emitted from the spot where the vial had struck.

"Give me another one, Gordy! I'm out of ammo!"

"Would you stop it?" Gordy slapped his hand away. Using Max's shoulder as a support, he stood up against the wall.

Bawdry took a shaky step forward, testing his weight against the floor.

Gordy gripped the other vial of Torpor Tonic, aimed, and launched. The bottle hit home, striking the mummy in the chest, green fumes enveloping the creature's face.

"Nice shot!" Max cheered.

Bawdry staggered backwards, but instead of crumpling to the ground, unconscious, he shook away the fumes and snarled.

"What's going on down there?" Gordy's dad bellowed. "I can't move!"

"It's Bawdry!"

"What about him?"

"He's attacking us!"

Gordy heard his dad fighting against the tight knots of the rope. "Get out of there!"

Bawdry turned his head toward Gordy's dad's voice, and then he slid sideways over to the door, blocking their escape route up the stairs.

"What other weapons do we have?" Max held the flashlight like it was the hilt of a tiny, insignificant sword.

Gordy pulled the remaining two bottles of Torpor Tonic from his bag and threw them at Bawdry. He knew they wouldn't work, but it would serve as a distraction. While the mummy batted away the green cloud, Gordy raced across the room to the center apothecary table where his mom kept multiple vials of potions at the ready.

"Max, get over here!" Gordy demanded.

"Are you crazy?" But he was already on his way to Gordy's side.

"Start reading off labels." Gordy crammed half a dozen bottles into Max's hands.

"Okay, uh, this one says Goi-lican-je—" Max squinted. "I can't read this."

"Forget that one. It's Bosnian tickling juice." Gordy activated one of the Bunsen burners and furiously tossed ingredients into a small cauldron. The mixture roiled angrily beneath the growing flame.

"Tickling?" Max shrugged and then chucked the bottle at the mummy.

"I told you to forget that one," Gordy said.

"It can't hurt, can it? I hate getting tickled."

Upon impact, the Goilicanje Juice spread across Bawdry's shoulders. His body began to twitch and convulse, and to Gordy's surprise, it succeeded in slowing him down.

"What else?" Gordy demanded, gritting his teeth in concentration.

"Gran . . . gou . . . Gruel—"

"Don't throw that one." He pulled it from Max's fingers and set it carefully on the counter. "That will just make him hungrier. Move past the *G*s!"

Bawdry closed the distance. Gordy could still hear his dad struggling to break free upstairs, but he would never get out in time. This was about to end badly for everyone involved unless Gordy could stop it.

"Max, don't worry about Bawdry. Keep reading!"

"I think this one's called Oighear Ointment."

"Perfect!" Gordy grabbed the vial and emptied it into his mixture.

"Do you even know what you're doing?"

"I hope so. What's that one right there?" Gordy pointed to a large flask filled with white, glue-like liquid.

"It's called Blogu." Max turned the flask over to look for other writing. "It's Blogu . . . Goo."

Gordy grabbed the Blogu and dumped it into the cauldron. He slid open a drawer and pulled out a pair of gloves. They were a bit large for his hands, but they would have to do.

"Stand back!" he warned. Then, while alternating between stirring with his left and right hands, Gordy reduced the heat to the Bunsen burner. The mixture began forming a smooth, glossy ball. It looked clear, like ice, and emitted an extremely cold vapor. With the gloves protecting his skin, Gordy lifted the ball out of the cauldron. He waited for Bawdry to draw closer to the counter, and as the mummy reached out, trying to grab one of them, Gordy tossed the ball then immediately dropped to the ground, yanking on Max's arm.

Max fell beside him, and the two boys shielded their faces from the explosion.

Bawdry stood frozen, a thick shield of ice encapsulating him. His arm was still outstretched, reaching for Gordy, but he was unable to move an inch. The only parts of his body not solidified were his head and his left hand just below his wrist. Along the floor, streaks of clear ice splayed out from the mummy's feet like strands of a frozen spiderweb. Bawdry's fingers wiggled feverishly as though he was pounding the keys of an invisible piano, and his one eye flitted back and forth between Gordy and Max as the boys sidestepped around the table out of range.

"That was awesome!" Max held his hand against his chest, breathing hard. "What do you call that? Ice ball?"

"I don't know." Gordy shrugged. "I just made it up. I wasn't one hundred percent positive what it would do."

"You made that up just now? On the spot?" Max stared at Gordy in amazement.

"Those were all finished potions I used. I wasn't even sure if they could be combined. It was pretty risky."

"Wow!" Max whispered in awe. He blew out his cheeks. "Ice ball. You should definitely call it ice ball."

"Gordy!" Gordy's dad screamed. "Are you okay?"

During all the commotion, Gordy had forgotten his father was still strapped to the chair upstairs. "We're fine, Dad!"

"What about Bawdry?"

"He's fine too," Max answered.

"That's not what I meant!"

"He can't hurt us," Gordy said. "Just give us a minute."

"All right, but just know that I'm unable to move." Gordy's dad grunted, and the struggle continued as he attempted to break free.

"Those were really good knots," Gordy said to Max.

"Yeah, I guess. I just started tying things. Didn't really know what I was doing. I can't believe Bawdry's the one who's been sneaking around and destroying your house."

"Once the ice melts, he'll attack us again, unless we can stop him." Gordy slid behind Bawdry. The mummy's skin and bandages appeared magnified by the layer of ice. Water dripped down and pooled beneath him.

"How are we going to do that?" Max asked.

"For starters, we have to figure out how he came back to life and then we can figure out how to keep him from doing it again."

"How long will he stay frozen?" Max hesitantly reached out and grazed his finger over the ice.

"Not long. Fake ice melts much faster than the real

stuff." Gordy walked over to the body bag. "I don't know how Esmeralda got to him. It's not like we take Bawdry on walks. He's always wrapped up in his bag."

"Maybe your dad did it when he was Blotched," Max said.

Gordy had already considered that possibility. Having his dad as Esmeralda's personal servant gave her plenty of advantages as well as access to all areas of the house, including the lab.

"But how?" Gordy peeled up Bawdry's bag, searching for any object that didn't belong. "Reanimation potions are really high-level stuff. I don't even think my mom has instructions on how to make them in any of her books."

"There would have had to have been some sort of hand off the other day at the grocery store," Max pointed out.

"Okay," Gordy agreed. "But how do they keep controlling Bawdry? This sort of thing would require them to constantly be around to smear a potion onto him. And my dad's been back to normal for more than a day now." He chewed on his thumbnail. What could Esmeralda and Yeltzin have used to keep Bawdry constantly under their control? Did they somehow have another way into the lab? Maybe through a vent or an unprotected crack in the wall?

"All I know is that the ice is not covering up his stench." Max crossed the room and plucked the can of air freshener from the table.

Gordy watched him vigorously shake the aerosol can and then point the nozzle at Bawdry's opened mouth.

"The air freshener! Don't spray it!" The answer came surging into Gordy's memory. "My dad bought it at the same grocery store where he saw Esmeralda and Yeltzin. I'll bet you anything that can has been tainted. Quick! Bring it to me."

Gordy pulled out his bottle of Detection Spray. Keeping the can at a safe distance, he doused the nozzle with a heavy dose of pink liquid. The can immediately popped and fizzed and tipped over on its side.

Max ran his hands through his hair. "They thought of everything!"

A woman's laughter suddenly echoed through the room. "No sense in continuing this charade any longer. Now we can get down to business," the woman said.

Gordy recognized the strong English accent and spun around, holding the air freshener out like a weapon. "How did you get in here?"

Another burst of laughter.

Esmeralda's voice was clear and frightening, but Gordy could not locate where she was hiding.

"We've been here for a while now. Watching you sleep. Rummaging through your personal effects."

Max grabbed Gordy's sleeve and pointed to where Bawdry stood frozen. "The mummy," he whispered.

"What about him?" Gordy whispered back.

"He's talking!"

Bawdry's jaw appeared to move along with every word Esmeralda spoke. "I watched you make that brilliant ice concoction just now. That's far too difficult for a simple Dram to master."

Gordy felt his stomach churn as the two of them walked across the room and stood in front of Bawdry.

"Well, hello there, children. Are we having fun, yet?" Bawdry asked with Esmeralda's voice.

"Yuck!" Max retched. "You didn't tell me Esmeralda was a corpse."

Bawdry's eye focused on Max. "Very cute. But the mummy is just a device. One of many I have at my disposal."

"Then where are you really?" Gordy asked.

Esmeralda clucked her tongue. "Don't you worry. We are in close proximity of the house."

"What do you want?" Gordy demanded.

"You know what we want," Esmeralda answered. "But you've hidden it well. This could've been so much easier. We've stayed longer than we would've hoped to in this dreadful neighborhood."

"You want the potion," Gordy said.

"I want the Eternity Elixir. Now, be a good chap, and go and fetch it for us."

The Eternity Elixir? Gordy had never heard that name before. "We're not giving you anything!" he said.

"The ice is melting," Esmeralda purred. "And Bawdry's surprisingly strong considering how rotten he's become."

"Then we'll just have to kill him!" Max pounded his fist into his hand.

"He's already dead. But if you do manage to reverse the reanimation spell, we have plenty of other means to accomplish our goal."

"If that was the case, why didn't you try something else to begin with? Why did you sneak around?" Max asked.

Bawdry's jaw creaked as he fought against the ice to look at Max. "Because none of you were to be involved. We didn't wish to harm you. You were not the enemy, but all that changed when you decided to meddle."

"It's gone!" Max blurted. "Your stupid potion. Gordy burned it all up."

Esmeralda's laughter was loud and boisterous, but Bawdry's mouth only opened a fraction, his teeth clomping together clumsily. "Burned it? You're good, Gordy Stitser, but not that good."

"Max is right," Gordy said. "I was trying to run a test and the whole thing went up in flames."

"Bring it to me," Esmeralda commanded.

"Are you deaf?" Max shouted. "There's nothing to bring."

"Insolent little brats!" Bawdry's hand suddenly shot out, shattering the ice. His bony fingers closed around Max's arm. Twisting and straining against his frozen prison, Bawdry forced the ice to break away from his neck and chest. Then, as his other arm came loose, the mummy clawed the rest of the ice off his body.

Max tried to pull away, but Bawdry wouldn't release

him. Gordy dove at the mummy's hand, but the grip was too tight.

"No Dram could have destroyed the Eternity Elixir. Now bring it to me, or I will do horrible things to this boy."

From upstairs, there was a crash of glass in the kitchen, more footsteps thundering on the floor, and then—

"Gordy!" Gordy's dad shouted. "Something's coming downstairs!"

CHAPTER

27

Max leaned backwards, trying to use his weight to force the mummy to release him. "What is that thing?"

The "thing" was a skeleton. Only it wasn't just a skeleton. There was something wrong with its head. In the place where a normal skull should've existed, the bony creature had an egg-shaped stone with a painted smiley face. Gordy wanted to scream, but he could only manage a high-pitched whine.

The skeleton never slowed as it descended, diving headlong into Bawdry with the force of a cannonball. The mummy smashed against the wall, his grip on Max's arm broken.

The two undead creatures then engaged in a wrestling match.

"Who sent you? Is this your handiwork, Priscilla?" Esmeralda demanded.

Bawdry grappled with the skeleton, working his arms

around the stone skull and forcing it into a headlock. The skeleton didn't respond. It made no sounds. No heavy breathing. Then again, Gordy wasn't sure if it could make sounds without a real skull to work with.

"It's a zombie death match!" Max screamed.

"This is a creative twist, I must say," Esmeralda continued shouting at the skeleton. "But you should've picked a more formidable warrior. I have you now!" Bawdry squeezed, tightening his hold around the skeleton's neck.

Gordy could see the skeleton struggling, unable to wiggle free. Suddenly, it hoisted Bawdry into the air and hurled him into the centrifuge. Vials of potions exploded, their contents mixing together and creating a wall of multicolored smoke.

Bawdry was down, but not out.

"We've got to get out of the lab!" Gordy shouted.

Keeping their eyes glued to the two battling creatures, Gordy and Max pulled their shirts up over their mouths, and ran up the stairs.

Brushing away bubbling liquid and broken glass, the mummy stood shakily and pointed a finger at Gordy. "Don't go too far," Esmeralda called out. Then Bawdry charged at the skeleton again. There was another crash as more glass shattered and potions sprayed.

Gordy and Max frantically untied the ropes around Mr. Stitser's arms and legs. The house was once again in a state of disarray. Glass from the living room window lay across the floor, along with soil from his mom's fern. A trail of thin, bony footprints tracked a path through the dirt.

Gordy stared at the jagged hole in the window and blinked. The skeleton must have had a long running start in order to propel it headfirst into the room. The footprints headed directly into the kitchen, but made a wide arc around his dad's chair.

"Get to the van!" Gordy's dad ordered. His voice was low, but his eyes were fixed with a determined stare on the door to the basement.

There was another violent crash from downstairs, an earsplitting cackle from Esmeralda, and then the lab grew deathly still.

Gordy felt his heart pounding in his throat. Was the fight over? Was there a victor, or had both undead creatures destroyed each other?

"Go, go, go!" Mr. Stitser pointed to the garage, but Max had beat him to the punch and was already slipping through the exit. Gordy stood rooted to the floor in the living room, watching the basement door and listening.

"Gordy! Come on!" his dad shouted.

"Wait!" Gordy insisted. There were still no sounds from down below. Nothing was climbing the stairs. Holding his breath, he inched toward the door, but his dad's hand closed around his arm, tugging him backwards.

"Get over here now, son! I'm not fooling around!"

"I have to check," Gordy resisted. "I think . . . I think we're safe now."

"How could you possibly know that?"

"Because nothing's coming up to get us." If Bawdry had won, the mummy would've already ascended the steps. Since nothing was climbing the stairs, it meant there was an excellent chance the skeleton had won. "Let me just look."

A car horn honked loudly, and Max's incoherent babble echoed from the garage.

Gordy's dad narrowed his eyes and sighed. "Okay, Gordo, we'll do it together."

The basement door creaked as they pushed it open. A reddish haze hung in the air over the steps. At the bottom, the skeleton stood, head bowed, motionless. As the door opened wider, the skeleton slowly looked up.

Mr. Stitser gripped Gordy's arms, ready to yank him out of harm's way.

Gordy swallowed. His whole body was trembling, but he didn't think they were in danger any more.

"What is that thing?" his dad asked.

"I don't know," Gordy answered. "But I think it's on our side."

CHAPTER

28

Raspy breathing and footsteps echoed down the otherwise silent street. Security lights above garage doors flickered on as the figure darted past. A neighbor's dog sniffed at the intruder's advance and scurried out of his doghouse, barking furiously. The dog pressed his muzzle against the chain-link fence and caught a glimpse of the thing making all the noise. The dog's barking instantly ceased.

The wind would eventually remove all evidence of Bawdry's trek through the neighborhood, but for the moment, his ashy footprints smudged the sidewalk as well as the corner of the Stitsers' roof, where the mummy had emerged from the chimney only moments before.

Bawdry hobbled to the end of the street, never looking in any other direction, a tail of unwound bandages flapping behind him like the end of a tattered scarf. He crossed the road, and the headlights of the car waiting at a stop sign lit up his whole body. The driver, who had been texting his girlfriend while the car idled, glanced up in time to see a blur of bandages as Bawdry disappeared into the shadows.

Finally, the mummy arrived at his destination. The back door of the white SUV opened, and Bawdry climbed in, plopping down on the leather seat with a squish. He took two quick breaths, and then the force controlling him left his body. His one eye glazed over, and his jaw went slack.

"What's he doing here? He's gooey, no?" Yeltzin asked, peering over the headrest. The sounds of Russian classical musical poured out of the radio. Esmeralda sat next to Yeltzin in the passenger seat, her fingers pressed against her temples, and her eyes clamped shut. She exhaled through her nostrils, unclasped her leather satchel, and pulled out a vial of muted orange liquid.

"He's going to ruin upholstery," Yeltzin said. "And he smells unpleasant."

"Please be quiet, moron, I have a splitting headache," Esmeralda said, after downing the orange antidote. "That didn't go exactly as planned."

"What happened?" Yeltzin turned the volume down on the radio. "You kept twitching, and your lips were moving, but no sounds came out."

"The boy knows of our intent," she answered. "As does Wanda."

Yeltzin removed the foil wrapping on a stick of gum and stuck it in his mouth. "So what? We thought they might have suspicion."

"There's no suspicion any more. Believe me, they know."

"How?" He chewed noisily on the gum.

"Because I spoke to Gordy. And because I was attacked by a revivified skeleton that was sent to protect him."

Yeltzin stopped chewing. "What? Is that why mummy is now passenger here?"

"I don't have time to explain everything to you." Esmeralda rummaged once more in her satchel. The contents of bottles sloshed, but instead of a potion, she brought out her cell phone. "We need to alert everyone immediately. Take us back to the hotel. I need to gather all my supplies. I don't know how much time we have before the Board sends help to the Stitsers."

"But I thought you said Wanda would never involve B.R.E.W. in this matter." Yeltzin shifted into drive and eased down on the gas pedal. The SUV lurched forward.

"Wanda wouldn't, necessarily, but that won't stop her son or her husband from reporting it."

"They would know who to contact?"

"Would you stop asking questions and drive faster!"

Yeltzin stomped on the gas pedal. The SUV sped up, and Bawdry's now-lifeless body toppled sideways onto a paper sack printed with the logo *Martin's Burgers*.

Yeltzin glanced into the rearview mirror and scrunched his face in disgust. "Ugh! I wasn't finished eating that. Now I'll have to toss it. Shame."

"Stop worrying about your stomach and start preparing yourself!" Esmeralda snapped. She typed a message into her phone and sent it to her contact list. "We attack the house before dawn."

I t's all clear. Bawdry's definitely gone," Mr. Stitser announced as he returned to the kitchen, closing the door to the basement lab behind him. "Went straight up the chimney. But the lab is destroyed."

Gordy breathed a sigh of relief. "Good. I mean not good that the lab's destroyed, but good that Bawdry has left. He shouldn't be able to come back anymore."

"Are we absolutely positive?" his dad asked.

Gordy shrugged. "I think so. The wards should work against him now that he's left."

Mr. Stitser nodded and turned his attention to the bony visitor. "What do we do about that? Max, stop poking it, please."

Max was busy waving his hand in front of the skeleton's painted-on face, snapping his fingers next to its stone skull, and flicking its ribs. "I don't think we can trust it, Mr. Stitser," Max said. "Skeletons are almost always evil."

"This one saved us from Bawdry and since its come up

here, it has tolerated you poking and pushing it nonstop," Gordy said. "I think it's definitely on our side."

His dad leaned against one of the tables and folded his arms. "Why don't you explain to me how you came to that conclusion."

"For starters, Esmeralda could tell it was sent from someone else," Gordy explained. "She mentioned Priscilla when they were fighting."

"So?" Max blurted out. "That doesn't prove anything."

"Okay, but what about the wards?" Gordy asked. "They've worked like they were supposed to, so far. Why was the skeleton able to break through the window? I think it's because it had permission from Mom. She's the only one who could give it."

Mr. Stitser headed for the stairs to the second level. "I'm grabbing a few things, and then we're out of here. We'll pick up the twins from Grandma and Grandpa Stitsers and then we'll stay in a hotel until Mom gets back." He nodded at Max. "We'll drop you off on the way."

Max flinched in surprise. "You're taking me home?"

"I don't think that's a good idea," Gordy said to his dad.

"Exactly!" Max snapped his fingers and pointed at Gordy. "You need me for protection. I stay cool and calm under pressure."

"That's not what I meant," Gordy said, puffing out his cheeks. "Our house is the safest place for everyone."

"You're not suggesting we stay here?" his dad asked,

laughing. "Look, I understand we're all very confused and shaken up by this, but I'm going to make the decision, and everyone needs to obey it. Understand?" Gordy's dad hurried up the stairs to his bedroom.

Gordy wanted to protest. He knew the only reason they had lasted as long as they had was because of the home wards. And the skeleton was still there, standing guard. At least, Gordy thought it was standing guard. He couldn't tell for sure considering the creature's face was drawn onto the stone head. It made it impossible to know what direction it was looking let alone what it might be thinking. This, by far, had been the most bizarre night of Gordy's life. A walking and talking mummy. A skeleton coming to their rescue. Max sleeping over on a school night.

Gordy stood in front of the skeleton. "Can you understand me?"

The skeleton tilted its head to one side.

"Do you think your mom can see you right now?" Max asked. "Like through its eyes?"

Gordy shook his head. "It doesn't have any eyes. They're drawn on."

"What do you think we should call it?" Max asked.

"Call it?"

"I think Slim is a good name." Max smiled. "Good Ol' Slim."

A knock sounded on the front door. Gordy and Max grabbed each other and then looked at the skeleton for help. It stood still and rigid, making no indication it had heard the knock.

"That was the door!" Max whispered.

"I know!" Gordy whispered back.

Another knock, louder than before followed by a soft voice. "Hello? Is anyone in there?"

Max yelped. "It's Yeltzin! Hey, Slim! Protect us!"

Slim didn't move.

Gordy eyed the door. Yeltzin was Russian, but the voice behind the door sounded very much American.

"No need to worry," the male voice said through the door. "I'm not an enemy. My name is Bolter, and I work with Wanda at B.R.E.W."

"Bolter?" Gordy headed for the door.

"Don't open it," Max said. "It's probably a trap."

Gordy had met Bolter at B.R.E.W. Headquarters. He was the weird guy with the mayonnaise jar and the missing fingers. What was he doing at the house?

"I'm not alone," Bolter continued. "I've brought someone with me who can help. Her name is Zelda, and we are both"—he paused—"friends."

Gordy tried to control his breathing and then spoke. "Why are you here?"

"Ah, is that you, Gordy? Very good. I've been made aware that your family has been dealing with some trouble as of late. We have simply come to provide assistance until Wanda's safe return."

"Why isn't the stupid skeleton doing anything?" Max

tossed a pillow toward Slim. "I think it's broken. I'm serious, Gordy. Opening that door is a big mistake. Mr. Stitser, there are crazy people at the door!"

Max was right. How could they possibly trust anyone? Gordy's own father had been easily Blotched by Esmeralda, which meant no one was safe.

"What's happening?" Gordy's dad bounded down the steps. "Who is it?"

Gordy pointed at the door, his eyes widening. "He says his name's Bolter and he works with Mom."

"He's lying," Max announced.

Gordy and his dad looked at Max, who had managed to wedge his body between the cushions of the couch.

"This is Mr. Stitser," Gordy's dad said sternly to the door. "It's very late, and I demand to know who this is." He glanced at Gordy and shrugged.

"Mr. Stitser, I apologize for the interruption, but I gather you haven't necessarily had what one would call a peaceful evening. Am I right?" the man asked. "My name is Bolter Farina. I work with your wife and have known her for many years. I am someone you can trust."

Gordy's dad ran his fingers through his hair and stared through the kitchen at the garage door as if contemplating an escape route. "I'm sorry, Mr. Bolter, but I don't think we can let you in," he said.

Gordy leaped back as the dead bolt suddenly twisted on its own. Before he could react, the chain lock unlatched and the door pushed open an inch.

"They're coming in!" Gordy looked around desperately for some sort of weapon to protect himself and then at the skeleton.

The dark-skinned man stood in the doorway, a warm smile spread across his mouth. Standing beside him was a middle-aged woman with short green hair and white lipstick. She had white eyelashes that made her blue eyes glow in the porch light, and she wore an enormous gold hoop earring in her left ear.

Bolter looked exactly how he had the first time Gordy had met him. Tight blue jeans, a cream-colored sports jacket, and charcoal-gray goggles strapped to his forehead. He had pulled his long black hair back into a ponytail. Dangling from his gnarled hand was a medium-sized bag, which looked to be made from alligator skin.

"Don't scream or run. Again, unnecessary." Bolter calmly held up his hand.

Gordy took a shaky step backwards, and his dad stepped in front of him.

"You can't come in here!" his dad commanded.

"Please, please, calm yourselves," Bolter said. "No need to panic."

"The . . . the wards." Gordy meant to say it as a threat, but it came across as a cautious warning. Any second now, Bolter and his strange companion would spin around and head far away from the house. That was how the wards always worked.

"Attack, Slim! Attack!" Max hopped up and down on

the couch, clinging to a throw pillow like a shield. But the skeleton refused to obey any commands.

"The wards won't work against us, I don't believe," Bolter said.

"Explain yourself quickly, Bolter," the green-haired woman said. "They look ready to make a run for it." Her high-pitched voice sounded as though she had sucked in all the helium from a balloon.

"I see you must've been through a lot lately, and I apologize for any alarm we have caused," Bolter said. "We've been invited to your home."

"By who?" Max asked.

Bolter looked over Gordy's shoulder and pointed at the skeleton. "By him."

30

So there I was, working in my shop at home, minding my own business when out of nowhere, this fine fellow suddenly started knocking on my window." Bolter gestured to the skeleton with his nubby hand and laughed before reclining on the couch and sipping his tea. "I must say I was a bit befuddled."

Gordy's dad returned from the kitchen with another cup of tea. He offered it to Zelda, who was busy attempting to tidy up the living room.

"What's in it?" she asked in her squeaky voice.

"Tea, lemon, and some sugar," Gordy's dad said.

"You don't happen to have any milkweed nectar, do you?"

Mr. Stitser puffed out his cheeks and looked at Gordy for an answer.

Gordy shrugged. "We do . . . er, did, but it's downstairs in that mess."

Zelda twirled her finger. "Don't bother. I'm not thirsty."

"Anyway," Bolter continued, "our bony friend left

immediately to monitor your home while I stopped to gather a few supplies and bring Zelda along for the ride. We came as quickly as we could, but, by the looks of things, we didn't come fast enough."

"And you let a skeleton into your home?" Gordy sat cross-legged on the floor next to the coffee table, listening to Bolter's story. "Just like that?"

Bolter blew across his teacup. "I saw no need to be alarmed."

"But he's a skeleton!" Max sat beside Gordy plunging vanilla cookies into his cup of tea until they were sopping and spongy.

"But he was so polite and reserved. It would be rude of me not to at least acknowledge him. In my line of work, I see all sorts of odd things from time to time. How was I to know it wasn't one of my colleagues suffering from an unfortunate accident? Was I simply to ignore him based upon my initial observation of his appearance? Plus, he carried this with him." Bolter reached into his jacket pocket and produced a piece of paper. He unfolded it and read the writing scribbled across the sheet.

Dearest Bolter,

Please help my family. They may be in dire circumstances. And trust the skeleton. His name is Doll.

Sincerely,
Wanda Rook Stitser

"His name's Doll?" Max looked disappointed. "That's lame."

"I called Wanda and confirmed it on the way over here from Zelda's," Bolter said.

"Called her?" Gordy's dad asked. "How? We haven't been able to get through to her on her cell phone. It goes straight to her voice mail."

"That's because she's somewhere far out of range of a cell tower and normal phone services, but I have this." Bolter once again reached into his sports coat, but this time he pulled out an enormous, brick-shaped cell phone. A foot-long antenna rose up from the top. Instead of buttons, a dial with numbered slots rested at the center of the phone. He inserted his knuckle into one of the slots and began dialing. The phone made a grinding sound as the dial swiveled with each entered number, then Bolter pressed the receiver up to his ear. He cleared his throat and stared at the ceiling until the line connected.

"Hello, Wanda. I've arrived." Bolter smiled, listening to the person on the other end. "Yes, yes, they are all here . . . Wait—" He covered the bottom part of the phone and leaned toward Gordy's dad. "The younger children—are they all right?"

"They're at their grandparents for the night," Mr. Stitser answered.

Bolter nodded and returned to the call. "All is well. Would you like to speak to your family?" He nodded again and then pressed a button and placed the phone on the coffee table.

"Hello? Gordon?" The magnified sound of Wanda Stitser's voice poured from the receiver.

"Yes, dear, it's me," Gordy's dad replied.

"Are you all right?"

"We're hanging in there."

"Good," she said, clear relief in her voice. "And who's with you? Gordy, are you there?"

"Mom," Gordy said, choking back tears. He couldn't help it. Hearing his mom's voice brought on a wave of both relief and sadness. He needed her home right now. How much longer were they supposed to hold out against Esmeralda?

"And Max!" Max added.

"Oh, Max," Wanda said fondly. "I have to admit I am surprised to learn you are staying over on a school night, but it's good that you're there, supporting my son."

"What's happening, Mom?" Gordy asked. "Why do these people keep trying to get into our house?"

"Please tell me you received a package from your Aunt Priss," Wanda said, desperation in her tone. "It contained a vial of the utmost importance."

"I don't think so—" Gordy's dad began.

"Yes, we did," Gordy said, averting his eyes from his father. "The vial is upstairs safe in my room. I'm sorry, Dad. I should have told you." He felt his cheeks flush. This was not the way he wanted his dad to find out. Gordy had planned to tell him, but so much had happened over the past few days.

"Why didn't you tell me?" Mr. Stitser asked, folding his arms.

"My guess is he suspected you were Blotched," Bolter suggested. "In which case, it was wise to withhold that bit of information, don't you think?"

Mr. Stitser's head bobbled in agreement. "Yeah, you're probably right."

Gordy ran his finger over the spot where the other potion had stuck him. "Mom, there was something else in Aunt Priss's package and it pricked me." He remembered how the vial had mysteriously filled up with red liquid that looked like blood. His blood.

His mom sighed. "Yes, it was your aunt's Confirmation potion. A way for her to know the Elixir made it into the right hands."

Gordy blinked in disbelief. "So, she wanted to send it to me?"

"No. Not at all. You were never meant to handle that vial."

Gordy stared at the floor. "I'm sorry, mom. I should have never opened that box."

"There's no time to discuss this now," Gordy's mom replied. "I trust you've met Esmeralda Faustus."

"Yes, we did," Gordy's dad said. "And she's not alone. Her partner's a man named Yeltzin. And they somehow controlled Bawdry to attack us."

"But we stopped him," Max added. "With an ice ball."

"Esmeralda is looking for the Eternity Elixir," Gordy said, ignoring Max. "Why does she want it so badly? What does it do?"

"Listen to me, Gordy. I've saved the last of my phone's battery for this conversation, and I'm afraid I have only minutes left. Esmeralda's not finished. She will return with reinforcements. Possibly before morning. They are planning to destroy B.R.E.W. With the Elixir, they'll have what they need to accomplish their goal. If B.R.E.W. goes down, everything stops."

"What do you mean *stops*?" Gordy asked.

"There are horrible people out there, Elixirists who were banished for the most heinous crimes. The downfall of B.R.E.W. will result in their immediate freedom. You must do all that you can to keep the Eternity Elixir from Esmeralda."

"Wanda, what are you suggesting we do?" Gordy's dad asked.

She sighed. "Hide it somewhere safe, but don't put your lives in danger. The wards will hold for a while, but if they start to crack, get out of there."

"Should we go now?" his dad asked.

"No, you'll be safer behind the protection of the wards. That's why I've asked Bolter and Zelda to help out. They're very good at what they do."

"Never fear, Wanda," Bolter said, winking at Gordy. "We shall keep that potion out of the hands of our enemies."

"Mom?" Gordy asked. "This potion? Is it something we can use against them?"

"Absolutely not, Gordy," his mom said. "Do not take any chances with that vial. When I get back, I plan to destroy it once and for all."

Gordy immediately felt a weight lift from his shoulders. He had already succeeded in burning the potion, which meant he had actually done something right.

"There's something I need to tell you." Gordy's heart raced. Maybe they had already won. Once Esmeralda discovered the truth about the Eternity Elixir, she would have no choice but to abandon her plans of destroying the Stitser home searching for it. All she would find would be an empty vial.

"I've run out of time," Wanda said. "I'm trying to get home from Greenland, but there's a horrible storm. The moment it lets up, even just a little, I'll be on the next flight home. I promise!"

"About that, Wanda," Zelda chimed in. "I checked my sources for precipitation in your area like you asked me to do."

"And?" Wanda asked, her voice rising.

"Blue skies and cloud free."

Wanda went silent on the other end. All Gordy could hear was the fizzing of poor cell phone reception. Finally, she replied, "I understand."

Then the line went dead.

CHAPTER

31

The blizzard raged. There seemed to be no end in sight, and in the midst of it all, the wind carried a haunting howl across the frozen landscape. It sounded like an injured animal, wailing in agony.

Wanda stood with her hand stretched beyond the mouth of the cave, collecting the stinging flakes in her palm. Her phone call had ended with her family and though they were surviving, Wanda was not at peace.

"How does it look?" Mezzarix slinked up next to her. He narrowed his eyes and stared out at the abyss of gray. "Any signs of it letting up?"

Wanda turned her head and smiled at her father. "Oh, yes," she answered coolly. "I can see the end of it."

"That's good! Soon you'll be—" But Mezzarix never finished his sentence.

Priscilla pounced from behind and doused her father with a bottle of Torpor Tonic. The old man slumped to his knees, unconscious.

"Grab him! Quick!" Wanda shouted. "He won't stay under long."

Priscilla bent down and picked up his feet. Wanda grabbed his hands, and the two of them hoisted his heavy, limp body over to the table. Bowls and cups scattered as Wanda cleared an area, and they dropped Mezzarix with a loud thud.

"Why did you do that?" Mezzarix groaned, reaching up with his hand to massage his temples.

Wanda answered by pouring another vial of Torpor Tonic into his mouth. Once again, Mezzarix fell limp.

"That was less than two minutes!" Priscilla said, breathless. "How many more do you have?"

"One," Wanda said. "Grab something to tie him up with. But don't use any potion other than the Torpor Tonic. He's too powerful for anything else."

Priscilla hurried to the other side of the cave. She tossed books and chairs. Metal cauldrons clanged as she brushed them aside.

"Hurry, please!" Wanda held the last vial of Torpor Tonic at the ready. She didn't know how much damage repeated doses of the powerful knockout agent would cause to her father, but right now she didn't care. If he woke up before they had him secured, they were both in serious danger.

"Aha!" Priscilla cheered and held up a length of gnarled rope. She hurried back to Wanda, and they worked together to tie Mezzarix securely to the table.

No sooner had they tightened the final knot than their father groaned in pain and blinked his eyes open. "Are we finished, yet? I can think of no worse activity."

"If you don't want me to dump the rest of the contents of my bag on top of you, you will start answering my questions immediately," Wanda snapped.

Mezzarix's nostrils flared with annoyance. "Fine."

"The storm?" Wanda asked. "It's not real, is it?"

"No," he answered dryly.

"You Blotched us?" Priscilla asked. "Where's the tainted object?"

Mezzarix sighed. "It's the wooden cooking spoon." He pointed with his chin over to the pot of stew.

Priscilla grabbed the spoon, and Wanda removed three small packets of multicolored powder from her satchel. She sprinkled each packet onto the spoon in succession and then gripped the handle in her fingers.

All at once, the raging storm vanished. In its place, a serene landscape of melting snow and mountain stone appeared. Sunlight crept through the cavern, warming everything it touched. The air was still bitter cold, but the sudden, unexpected warmth made it seem almost like summer.

"How long have you been working with Esmeralda?" Wanda asked.

Mezzarix raised one of his silvery eyebrows. "Define *working with.*"

Priscilla squeezed her arms tightly at her chest. "How?

I don't understand how she could even know you're still alive. Greenland was the last inhabitant-free Forbidden Zone. There aren't coordinates or markers on any map at B.R.E.W. We were so careful! It doesn't make any sense!"

"Relax, Priss," Mezzarix soothed, running his tongue across the front of his teeth and suppressing a chuckle. "It's not what you think. In truth, I really don't know Esmeralda that well. I knew her parents and some of her relatives years ago—a bunch of crazies to be certain. But I'm not in cahoots with the Faustuses."

"Then why are you helping them?" Priscilla asked. "Why did you keep us here?"

Mezzarix gave a slight shrug. "Opportunity knocked, and I simply opened the door. If Esmeralda succeeded in destroying the Vessel, I would be free to walk away from this dreadful mountain."

"You've endangered the lives of your grandchildren for your own gain?" Wanda said. "You are truly despicable!"

"Don't say that." Mezzarix pouted. "Your family is safe because of my help. Besides, I've changed my mind. I don't want Esmeralda to acquire the Eternity Elixir anymore. She seems too rash. Too violent. The Elixir should not end up in her hands."

"Ha!" Priscilla smacked the table. "You're only saying that because you don't want us to leave you tied up in this cave."

"Nonsense, dear Priss. I freed myself from these bindings the moment I woke up." Mezzarix wiggled his arms, and the coils of rope dropped to the floor. "It's a bothersome talent I have, I know."

Both women leaped away from the table. Wanda squeezed the vial of Torpor Tonic in her hand, but Mezzarix remained on his back, his palms held up in submission.

"You see now that I am more powerful than the two of you combined. And should I wish ill towards either one of you, I could do as I please. But that's not what I want."

"What do you want?" Wanda asked.

"I want my family back. And if I have to remain in captivity here in Greenland, so be it."

"Come on, Wanda," Priscilla said, backing toward the cavern's opening. "We don't need his help."

"But you do," Mezzarix said. "You know you do. Who else will you take the Elixir to? B.R.E.W. Headquarters?" He clicked his tongue and grinned. "If it were that simple, you would've done so twelve years ago. But you felt you couldn't go to B.R.E.W. because you didn't trust they would be honorable in how they used it."

"Let's go!" Priscilla grabbed Wanda's arm.

But Wanda stood still, staring at her father. Everything he had said was true. Sure there were good Elixirists who worked at the headquarters, but none of them had encountered anything quite as powerful as the Eternity Elixir. If that potion fell into the wrong hands, like Esmeralda Faustus, there would be so much destruction.

"What are you proposing?" Wanda asked.

Mezzarix propped his body up with his elbows.

"I propose a trade. You have the ingredients to concoct an Axiom Application, I assume?"

Wanda glanced down at her bag, but faltered. "Why would we need that?"

"Because what I'm about to offer will seem like deception."

"Like everything else you've done," Priscilla said.

"Precisely. But I would like you to believe me. An Axiom Application should do the trick. Should there be any inkling of falseness in the deepest crevices of my mind, the Axiom would find it and reveal it to you." Priscilla was shaking her head, but Mezzarix held up a finger. "Wanda believes me. Don't you?"

"He's right." Wanda stared once more into her bag. "An Axiom Application is foolproof. What are you offering?"

"Simple. Should you succeed in vanquishing your foe and acquiring the Elixir, you shall bring it back here, and I shall destroy it."

Wanda licked her lips. "You won't try to use it to break free of your banishment?"

Mezzarix moved his finger over his chest, crossing his heart. "Absolutely not."

"What are your terms in exchange for destroying the Elixir?" Priscilla asked.

The old man smiled. "Just another visit from Wanda. Within the year."

"That's it?" Wanda furrowed her brow.

"That's it." Then he smiled and his eyes widened. "As long as you bring Gordy along with you on that visit."

Wanda opened her mouth. "Bring Gordy?"

Mezzarix nodded. "Yes. That is his name, is it not?"

"You want me to bring my oldest son to the most dangerous Scourge ever to terrorize the potion community?"

"No." He waved his hand dismissively. "I want you to bring your oldest son to his grandfather. And I promise you, on my life, no harm will come to him." He swung his legs over the side of the table. "We will just visit, with your supervision. I will share grandfatherly advice, and then I will destroy the Eternity Elixir." He brushed his hands together. "And the Axiom Application will testify of my honest intent."

Wanda turned away, and Priscilla drew in close next to her. "You're not seriously considering bringing Gordy, are you? After all Dad's done?"

Wanda covered her mouth with her hand and fought back the urge to cry. "He wasn't always a horrible man, Priss. I don't want to go through this anymore. If we destroy the Elixir, then we're free of it." She turned back around. "All right. We'll make the deal. As long as you agree that after we've destroyed the Elixir, both me and my son are free to leave forever."

"If that's what I have to live with, I'll take it."

32

Glass from at least a hundred shattered vials crackled under Gordy's feet. His mom's drying rack had collapsed, the herbs reduced to mulch. The swirling fragrance of spilt potions and trampled substances smelled more like a wickedly brewed cup of hot and sour soup. It was tingly and pungent, with undertones of ginger, maple syrup, and just a hint of battery acid.

Gordy held a handkerchief to his mouth, but kept his nose uncovered. He needed his ability to Decipher in order to know whether or not he was headed into a noxious cloud. So far, despite the cringe-inducing scents, the lab appeared to be safe. Gordy could hear his dad upstairs, discussing plans with Bolter and Zelda. The home wards would hold for a bit, but Bolter agreed with Mr. Stitser that the sooner they devised a clear route out of the neighborhood, the better. Gordy's dad was handling things well for not having much experience in the way of potion-making.

Max stood on the stairs, retching. "Zip it up already!" he demanded, pointing to Bawdry's empty body bag.

Gordy glanced at his friend. "That's not the problem, I promise you."

"Just do it, okay?"

Gordy rolled his eyes and wove his way through the mess. He knelt down and zipped the plastic container closed.

"Smells better already," Max said, sighing in relief. "What are we looking for anyway?"

"Anything worth salvaging," Gordy said.

There was so much destruction in the lab. He felt sick for his mother's loss. Years of accumulating ingredients had been destroyed in a three-minute, undead grudge match. The canary bellflower lay in a trampled heap. That plant had been a permanent fixture in the lab as long as Gordy could remember, and now it was gone. He stooped over it and delicately ran his fingers over the flower's withered bloom. Gordy gritted his teeth and swore that he would make Esmeralda Faustus pay for what she had done.

As he stood, staring silently at the canary bellflower as if holding a candlelight vigil, Gordy's eyes drifted toward the center apothecary table and the bottom left-hand drawer. The one marked VOLATILE. The one Gordy had been forbidden to ever open. The one now slightly ajar, its lock broken.

Dusting his hands on his pant leg, Gordy approached the table and held his breath as he slowly opened the drawer. Part of him thought he should wait for his mother to come home, but what if there was no house to come home to? What if Esmeralda attacked and destroyed everything else? Maybe, Gordy thought, just maybe, that drawer contained a weapon. Something to protect the Stitsers against Esmeralda and her Russian thug.

Having brewed for several years now, Gordy assumed he had seen all there was to see in the potion community. He had worked with unstable substances, harvested thorn-riddled plants dappled with questionable sap, and even milked the fangs of poisonous snakes, all while under the close supervision of his mother. And yet this drawer would be different. He would see items only seasoned Elixirists knew about. Gordy half-expected something hairy or tentacled to scurry out of the hole. But instead of vials cloaked in secrecy or concoctions of a sinister nature, the drawer was empty save for a single folded document.

"What is that?" Max asked, from above Gordy's shoulder. "Looks like a map."

It was a map. Gordy could tell that much from unfolding the first crease and seeing the crudely drawn lines etched upon the thick parchment. The paper felt old and oily. A few words had been scribbled on the map, but Gordy recognized one immediately.

Chicxulub.

The sketched images pinpointed the location of something in Mexico. Adilene had been right. The asteroid crater was of the utmost importance, though it was still cloaked in mystery.

Gordy sniffed the paper, closed his eyes, and allowed his skill to take hold. He sensed the ingredients of the parchment. He smelled wood pulp, bleach, rosin, and clay. Gordy could also pick up the ink composition used in forming the boundaries and borders of the hand-drawn map: propyl alcohol, iron, and a cellulose dye. But Gordy detected something else. Another ink had been used. One mixed with the toxic saliva from a blue-ringed octopus in order to write hidden messages.

Gordy's mind raced as he stood and cleared an area on top of the apothecary table. He smoothed out the map and then scanned the floor in search of what he needed. The lab was such a mess, Gordy doubted he'd be able to find anything, but luckily for him, not all the vials had been crushed. Gordy picked his way through broken glass and pieces of cork until he found a stoppered bottle of bar-bary fig needles and a Tupperware container of hawk eyes. Gordy combined the two in a pewter cauldron and ignited a Bunsen burner beneath it.

"I'm guessing you're—" Max started to say, but Gordy cut him off.

"This potion needs complete silence," Gordy said, his tone serious. "No talking, please."

Max didn't object, and Gordy continued with his mix-ing. Within a few seconds, the burner had reached the opti-mal temperature and Gordy added the final ingredient—a ripped corner of the map—into the cauldron. He then took a paintbrush and applied copious amounts of the mixture all over the parchment.

"I knew it!" Gordy said, his excitement growing as a hidden message appeared across the paper. There were two paragraphs separated by a pair of reddish thumbprints pressed beneath the first block of print. Gordy held the paper closer to the Bunsen burner for light and read the cursive script.

> For his Heinous Crimes committed against the Potion Community and for his creation of the Eternity Elixir, we, Wanda Rook Stitser and Priscilla Isering Rook, on this, the twenty-second day of October, do hereby Banish our father, Mezzarix Oleander Rook, the self-proclaimed Scourge of Nations, to Mont Forel, Sermersooq, Greenland. We seal this Banishment with our blood, thus rendering his abilities of Concocting, Brewing, and Philtering potions Void of Substance. In the Forbidden Zone, Mezzarix shall live out his Banishment until the End of his Days.

"What?" Gordy whispered, as he tried to process what he had just read. His grandpa was a potion master? He had never heard the name Mezzarix before, but the document had been written by either Gordy's mother or his Aunt Priss, and they named Mezzarix as their father.

Gordy lowered the paper and swallowed. "He's not dead?"

"Who's not dead?" Max asked.

"My grandfather." Gordy gazed in the direction of the fireplace, his eyes unfocused. Not only had his grandpa *not* died in a tragic farming accident, but he was still alive and, judging by what his mother had written, a dangerous criminal as well. An Elixirist gone bad. Why hadn't she told him? Gordy recalled the black-and-white photograph of his Grandpa Rook. The one he kept in his closet.

"Mezzarix," Gordy whispered, glancing back down at the document. He assumed the red thumbprints belonged to his mom and Aunt Priss. "Hey!" Gordy shouted as Max snatched the paper from his fingers. "You'll rip it!"

"I'm not going to rip it, but I can't just stand here while you zone out," Max said.

"Give it back to me. There is more to the message."

Max cleared his throat and read from the paper. "'The Eternity Elixir is impossible to destroy by any means we possess. As far as we know, it is the only self-replicating potion in existence.'" He scrunched his nose. "Self-replicating?"

"Let me read it, please." Gordy calmly held out his hand and Max gave him back the paper. Narrowing his eyes in concentration, Gordy finished reading the words his mother had written twelve years ago.

We don't know what Devilish Means our father used to create the Eternity Elixir, but every attempt at Destroying it has Failed—Fire. Explosives. Volatile Substances. The Potion always returns to its Previous Form and always in its Original Vial. Something this Dangerous cannot be allowed to fall into the Wrong Hands, and we cannot Trust everyone among the B.R.E.W. Elite. The Chicxulub Crater will Protect it from even the Most Skilled Ciphers. We pray that our hiding place goes Unnoticed until we discover how to properly rid the World of this Abomination.

"Well?" Max asked eagerly. "What did it say?"

Gordy set the paper back onto the counter and stared at Max, his mouth dropping open slightly, but he didn't answer. Instead, he hurriedly refolded the paper, crammed it back into the drawer, and raced for the stairs.

Gordy didn't stop running until he crashed through his bedroom door. He heard voices hollering after him, demanding to know why he was running, but to Gordy it sounded as though his dad and Bolter were yelling from the bottom of a swimming pool.

Max lagged behind, breathing heavily as he stumbled into Gordy's room, but by then, Gordy had already pulled the small box containing the destroyed contents of Aunt Priss's Eternity Elixir from his secret hiding spot.

"You should go out for track," Max wheezed. "You're a lot faster than I would've guessed."

Gordy stared down at the package, his heartbeat throbbing in his throat, and then he slid off the lid.

Cream-colored liquid sluiced around in the bottle just as it had done before Gordy burned it to a crisp.

"Oh, no," he muttered. "I swear I burned it all. Didn't I?"

"I thought so," Max said, still panting.

Things like this didn't happen in the potion world.

Boiling substances for too long rendered them powerless. Heat and fire destroyed everything. There was no returning from a mistake like the one Gordy had made with the Eternity Elixir. Yet, just when he thought a disaster had been averted, Gordy found himself smack dab in the middle of danger once more.

"I don't understand. How can it still be here?" Gordy demanded.

"It is not by mere happenstance that particularly devious concoction has been labeled the Eternity Elixir," Bolter announced from the doorway.

Gordy jerked in surprise, holding out the vial as though he had been caught red-handed. "I thought I burned it all up," he said.

Bolter entered the room and knelt next to Gordy. "I haven't dealt much with this potion. Well, truthfully, I have never seen it before in my life. But Wanda explained the details to me ages ago. The potion takes time to replicate. Hours. Maybe even a day or two." Bolter opened the vial and passed it under his nose.

"But how?"

"I don't know that I could say," Bolter said. "I'm afraid this concoction is a lengthy stride beyond my expertise."

"What if he had broken the bottle?" Max asked.

"Pardon?" Bolter glanced up from his sniffing.

"If Gordy had shattered the bottle, where would the potion have shown up?"

Bolter curled his lower lip in thought. "Excellent

question. I suppose, had Gordy succeeded in demolishing the container, the Eternity Elixir would reform in its last known spot. Like in a cauldron on an apothecary table, for example. It is a mystery, but I can assure you that the potion would indeed return, one way or the other." Bolter picked up the box of Gordy's special potions from the hole in Gordy's closet. "What are these?"

"Nothing," Gordy answered quickly.

"They don't look like nothing to me." Bolter rotated one of the vials and read the masking tape label. "Rocket Vomit. Oh my! Do these actually work?"

"They're just things I've made. My mom would flip out if she knew I was hiding them." Gordy took the box from Bolter.

"Then you'd best gather them up and keep them on you. Anything that would make your mom flip out will most likely be useful tonight."

"I'll carry them," Max offered, a little too eagerly.

"I don't think so," Gordy said. "They're dangerous."

"Yeah, but your hands are going to be full holding knockout potions and stuff like that," Max said. "I need something to protect me."

"He has a point," Bolter said. He handed Max a leather pouch with slots perfectly shaped to carry glass vials. "Careful now, fumbling fingers aren't suggested. Now, before we leave this room, we need to devise a . . ." He stopped and cocked his head to one side.

Gordy could almost see Bolter's ear quivering as he

listened. Suddenly, the thin Elixirist scuttled to his feet as the sound of heavy footsteps thundered on the stairs. Gordy's dad, panting breathlessly, burst into the room, with Zelda close on his heels, her bright green hair standing on end.

"What's going on?" Gordy asked, scrambling to his feet.

"Doll is gone," his dad said.

"What? Why?" Max demanded.

"Through the window from which he entered," Zelda said. "Casual, as though on a stroll through the park."

"Can we call him back?" Gordy asked Bolter. He'd felt better with the skeleton standing guard.

"That creature's departure is the least of our problems," Zelda said, nodding at Bolter.

"Oh, dear," Bolter said, squeezing Gordy's shoulder. "They're here."

Then the front door exploded, and a whirlwind of insects flooded into the house.

CHAPTER

34

Giant millipedes, oozing slugs, and a horde of clicking cockroaches swarmed through the door. There had to be millions of them. The chirping of the cockroaches drowned out almost every other sound. Bolter and Zelda stood at the top of the stairs, shouting to each other, but Gordy couldn't make out what they were saying, despite standing right next to them. Gordy could barely hear his own voice.

Zelda plucked a glass bulb from inside her bag and tossed it up and down in her hand, testing its weight. The bulb was filled with dark red glop that looked like lava. Winding back, she flung the bulb into the swarm, and a section of insects immediately caught fire and vaporized, leaving behind a circular hole. The buzzing cacophony subsided for a moment as the remaining insects scattered from the intensity of the fireball. It only lasted a few seconds, but it was long enough for Bolter to race over and

divvy out three tiny bluish pills to Gordy, his dad, and Max.

"Swallow it!" Bolter shouted as the insects reformed into an enormous cluster.

Gordy didn't hesitate. He shoved the pill into his mouth, worked up some saliva, and swallowed. All at once, the insects' buzzing dimmed, and he could hear Bolter's voice speaking directly into his ear as though he were wearing headphones.

"Testing, testing. Can you hear me?" Bolter asked.

"Yeah, whoa!"

"Dude, we could use these to coordinate a water balloon attack on the girls' softball team," Max suggested. "We could hear each other from across the field!"

"Why are the insects not attacking us?" Gordy asked Bolter. So far, the bugs had remained in a singular mass hovering just above the doorway to the basement.

"They're not here to attack us," Zelda said, her voice coming through loud and clear in his ears. "They're here to remove the wards." She pointed, and Gordy watched as the bugs dove at the top of the doorway where Mrs. Stitser had applied the protective ward.

As soon as a group of the millipedes and cockroaches succeeded in lapping up a bit of the potion, they would fall dead to the ground, a shower of never-ending corpses fluttering down as the swarm dwindled. The slugs slurped potion until they morphed into quivering bulbs and then popped with a splatter of goo.

"Clever girl, this Esmeralda," Bolter said. "That ward is as good as gone!"

"There are other exits," Gordy's dad said. "We could head for the garage."

"Too late," Zelda said. "The garage is compromised. Acorn weevils made light work of that ward."

"They're coming in for certain. We'll need to fight." Bolter rummaged in his bag and pulled out his inventory of bottles. "I have three Torpor Tonics, a couple of Vintreet Traps, at least half a dozen Miedo vials." The glass bottles pinged together as he rapidly sorted them.

"What's Miedo?" Max whispered to Gordy, while Bolter continued counting.

"It's a fear tonic. It makes you afraid of everything," Gordy said.

Max raised his eyebrows. "Can you make that?"

"Probably."

"Sweet!"

"And a tube of Purista." Bolter noted Max's dumb-founded look. "Finnish Squeezing Powder. You'll never want to be hugged like that." Bolter glanced at Zelda. "That's all I have, though. How about you? Did you bring weapons?"

"No need to worry about me," she said cryptically. "I have brought a few bitties."

Bolter leaned over and muttered to Gordy and Max. "Zelda works exclusively with explosives."

Max's mouth formed an "O," and he seemed to watch the green-haired Elixirist with newfound admiration.

"Oh, Gordy!" A shrill voice with an English accent echoed through the hall. "You no longer have wards to keep us out, and we have the house surrounded. We'll be taking the Elixir now, without any further fuss."

Mr. Stitser wrapped his arms around Gordy's chest and pulled him close as they listened to Esmeralda.

"You have held out long enough. Place the Elixir on the floor by the front door. You may then run and hide and await our departure. We do not wish to harm any of you. I do not care who brings me the Elixir, but see to it that it happens promptly." Esmeralda spoke with a lively tone. Gordy wasn't sure how many people were on her side, but he knew they were outmatched. "These are my terms. So what have you? Who's going to bring me my prize?"

Zelda responded by hurling another bottle of lava down the stairs at the remaining insects.

There were shouts of surprise and anger as Esmeralda issued her next command. "Get them all!"

The window at the end of the hall next to Jessica's room imploded. Glass shards sprayed as a burly woman clambered through the opening. She had ratty brown hair and bright flushed cheeks. In her left hand, she carried a green bottle with an extra-long nozzle. Drawing the bottle like a gunslinger, the woman shot a spray of what looked like window cleaning fluid towards the Stitsers. Mr. Stitser shoved Gordy out of the way and took the spray in the chest.

"Dad, no!" Gordy screamed. Mr. Stitser's body went limp. He collapsed into Gordy's arms, forcing the two of them to the ground.

The woman pointed the spray bottle again, this time at Max. Before she could pull the trigger, a glass vial shattered at her feet and a web of vines sprouted out, snatching at her like a family of striking cobras.

"Oh, no, you don't!" the woman said, dropping her spray bottle and trying to retreat through the broken window. But Bolter's Vintreet Trap had her in its grasp. The vines coiled around her legs and continued until it entangled her whole body. Though she struggled against the trap, she could not break free.

"Is he . . . is he . . ." Gordy stared at his dad, unable to finish the sentence, overwhelming dread filling his chest.

"It was a concentrated dose of Torpor Tonic," Bolter said, briefly examining Gordy's dad. "He'll be fine in a few hours."

Zelda pulled two large flasks from her bag, one filled with gray liquid, the other with white. Yanking the stopper out of the white potion, she poured a puddle at the top of the stairs, then tossed the rest down to the bottom.

From what Gordy could see, the potion didn't seem to be doing anything.

"What is that?" Max asked.

Zelda puckered her lips. *"Silex et Acier,"* she said with a French accent. "Flint and Steel." She uncorked the gray flask and frowned at Gordy. "You have a pretty home.

I feel dreadful about this. But . . ." She shrugged and then poured the gray liquid over the white potion.

An instant wall of flame shot up, filling the stairwell. Gordy could feel the intense heat and shielded his eyes with the back of his hand. The smoke detectors in the house unleashed a piercing alarm.

"That's no longer an optimal passage, don't you agree?" Zelda asked, before cackling like a witch.

"She's crazy!" Max said, cowering away from the flames.

"Oh, yes, definitely crazy and unstable," Bolter agreed. "Good thing she's on our side. We should carry your father into the closet."

With help from Bolter and Max, Gordy carried his dad into his bedroom and laid him gently on the floor in the closet. He could see his father breathing, and he felt a momentary sense of ease. But then the floor beneath his feet began to shake, and a hole opened in the center of the room. Gordy's dresser and desk were sucked into the opening, along with most of the carpet as dust and pieces of floorboard belched out from the opening.

"Might want to stay clear of that!" Bolter cautiously leaned over the hole to look down, only barely missing getting sprayed in the face with more of the concentrated green Torpor Tonic. "You wouldn't happen to have one of your Booming Balls, would you?" he called out to Zelda.

She stood in the hallway, admiring her wall of fire, and threw something at Bolter. It looked like a grenade.

Bolter caught it, pulled the pin, and tossed it down the hole.

There were more shouts and the sound of people scattering as the grenade exploded and released a column of hot-pink flames.

"You guys are going to burn down the whole house!" Gordy shouted. His mom's friends were out of control. Fire blazed in the hallway and rose up from the hole in the floor, casting intense heat into the room. What good would it do to defend the Eternity Elixir if Gordy's entire home burned up in the process?

"That wasn't our intent, I assure you," Bolter said, frowning guiltily. "We need to get you out of here. Is there another way to the main level?"

"Other than the stairs that are on fire?" Gordy answered. "I don't think so!"

Bolter's brow crinkled as he tapped his pursed lips. "Even if we do extinguish the fire, the stairs won't be stable enough to descend. We'll have to go through the hole."

Max dug his finger in his ear. "I think this isn't working, because it just sounded like he said we have to go through the hole. Am I the only one who can see that it's on fire?"

"Gordy, do you know how to construct a basic Dampening Draught?" Bolter asked.

Gordy nodded. "Yeah, and we probably have most of the ingredients in the bathroom."

"Good. Go fetch them. Max, help Gordy. I'll stay here and tend to your father."

Tend to his father? Gordy wanted to ask what that meant, but there wasn't any time. He and Max raced into the hall bathroom, shielding their heads against the heat. Gordy tossed Max a bath towel and instructed him to collect the items he would hand him. He grabbed mouthwash, toothpaste, and lotion. Cotton balls, triple-antibiotic ointment, and aspirin. Gordy filled a cup with tepid water from the tap and added three drops of hair conditioner.

"Oh, no!" Gordy searched desperately under the sink. "We don't have any Dragon's Blood! I thought we did. You don't have any, do you?" he asked Max.

"Like a real dragon's blood?" Max looked baffled.

"No! It's just called Dragon's Blood because of how it looks. It comes from the Cinnabari tree from the Socotra archipelago in the Arabian Sea."

"And you actually think I might have some of this Cinnabon stuff with me?"

Gordy groaned. "Without Dragon's Blood, I don't think this will work."

As they left the bathroom, they narrowly dodged the back draft of yet another Zelda explosion.

"Would you stop that already?" Gordy demanded.

Zelda cupped her hand over her ear. "Eh?" She hiccupped as two enormous hands seized her by the ankles. The gloved hands seemed to magically rise up from the carpet. They were followed by arms, shoulders, and then Yeltzin's smiling face.

"Hello, there! No more booming from you!" Yeltzin

proclaimed. Then he vanished through the floor, taking Zelda with him.

Max swallowed. "Oh, that's not good."

"We have a problem," Gordy said as he returned to the bedroom. "Zelda's gone. They got her."

Bolter frowned. "That's unfortunate, but she can take care of herself."

Gordy's eyes darted around the room. Something was wrong. "Where's my dad?" He noticed a bulging mound of blankets and sheets on the bed.

"Please control yourself." Bolter held up his hands to calm Gordy. "Your father, I assure you, is quite safe."

"What do you mean? Why have you wrapped him up like that?" Gordy patted the mound on the bed and felt his dad's large foot.

"I've cocooned him in a Tranquility Swathe. Are you familiar with how that works?"

"I think so, but what about the—"

"The Swathe will not only protect him from the elements but also from our enemies. Especially if we lure them away from the house."

Max ran his hands through his hair. "Are all Elixirists raving psychos?"

Bolter curled his lower lip in thought. "Pretty much. Now, what have you brought me?"

Gordy showed him the collection of ingredients. "We're missing Dragon's Blood. All my mom's supply is downstairs."

Bolter took the cup of water from Gordy and began

mixing. "No matter. Max, please guard the door. Alert us to the first sign of an intruder."

"Yeah, that was like a half an hour ago," Max complained, but he headed to the door anyway.

Bolter's nubby hands worked blindingly fast. He combined the conditioner and water with the toothpaste, alternating between stirring the concoction with his finger and a metal retractable wand he produced from his pocket. With his eyes closed, he shredded the cotton balls until they transformed into wispy gossamer fibers, which he doused with mouthwash. Though the potion was nearly complete, they were still missing the Dragon's Blood. Without it, they had nothing more than a goopy mess of toiletries.

"Gordy, hand me the Eternity Elixir," Bolter instructed.

Gordy uncorked the bottle and carefully placed it into Bolter's outstretched hand.

Max fell backwards. "Intruder! We have an intruder! They're coming through the fire!"

Bolter paid no attention to Max's alarm. He added one drop of the Elixir into his mixture and smiled. The potion gleamed with a glossy, sea-foam hue. Bolter took the cup filled with the Dampening Draught and poured it over the hole. There were only about ten to fifteen drops worth of liquid, but those instantly expanded, soaking the entire area and extinguishing the fire that had previously filled the hole. With the fire extinguished, there was no more time to waste. Gordy, Bolter, and Max leaped down to the floor below.

Gordy landed with a thud on the living room couch, or what was left of it. Zelda's grenade had incinerated all but the wooden frame and a single cushion. Tendrils of smoke rose up from the charred remains, and Gordy had to cover his mouth to stifle his coughing. The blaring of the smoke alarms continued, ringing in his ears. Surely, the neighbors would have heard it, not to mention the series of explosions. They would have called the police, or the fire department, or maybe even the National Guard.

As Gordy stood from the couch, strong hands grabbed him, forcing his arms behind his back. He glanced up and saw a man with a massive black beard and two tiny eyes blinking down at him. A cigar the size of a toilet paper tube jutted from the man's mouth, and pungent smoke coiled out from the tip.

"Don't struggle, boy," the man commanded. "I have no problem tearing off your arms after all you've done."

Who was this monster? Gordy noticed that a chunk of

the man's beard had been singed and a blackened blister bubbled on his cheek, compliments of one of Zelda's lava bombs, no doubt.

"Max, run!" Gordy called out. But as the smoke cleared, he saw his best friend wrestled to the ground by another enormous man, this one with long, red hair. The man grinned as he pinned Max, revealing a gleaming row of silver-capped teeth.

"Got you now. Nowhere to go, little boy. What will you do?" the man asked Max, hissing in his ear.

"I don't know. But what are you going to do with your face when Godzilla wants his butt back?" Max fired back, trying to shake free of his captor's grip.

The man holding Gordy snickered. "Good one, boy!"

Gordy looked for Bolter and found him lying face down on the floor, struggling against the tightening grip of a Vintreet Trap. Esmeralda stood with her foot firmly planted on his back.

"My, my, you have been quite the trouble. I know Gordy, and I recognize my good friend, Max," Esmeralda said, nodding at each of them. "But I haven't a clue who you are or your friend with the lovely green hair." She gave a sideways nod to a large mass of spiderwebs lying next to the television. Gordy could barely see the outline of a person beneath the webs.

"Let them go!" Gordy demanded, fighting against his captor.

"Hold him, Burke. He's a wild one," Esmeralda instructed.

Gordy felt the grip on his arms tighten. Gritting his teeth, he scanned the room in search of the rest of Esmeralda's followers. Were there only three of them? Four, if you counted the woman trapped upstairs. Where was Yeltzin? Gordy couldn't see the Russian anywhere, but still, that only made five. Had he known that was the extent of Esmeralda's army, perhaps they could have held out longer. Why had Zelda and Bolter resorted to exploding half the house?

"I trust there won't be any more surprises this evening." Esmeralda raised her eyebrows. "Anyone else we should be aware of upstairs?"

Gordy felt a ball of worry form in his stomach. His dad was upstairs, unconscious and wrapped up like a caterpillar in a chrysalis. What if Esmeralda suddenly got the urge to level the second floor? Shoulders slumping, Gordy shook his head.

"No one's up there," he muttered. "This is everyone."

Esmeralda walked away from Bolter, digging in her bag. "Good. You know, you could've avoided this." Climbing onto the recliner, she pulled out a bottle of Torpor Tonic and sprayed the smoke detector. The potion didn't completely stifle the shrill alarm, but the sound softened into dim, monotonous background noise.

"All the damage to your home. To your mother's lab. Look at this place!" Esmeralda flourished her hand around as she hopped off the chair, pointing out the smoldering remnants of the furniture. Potted plants lay overturned, and large segments of carpet had disintegrated, leaving only bare wood and scorch marks in their place. Gordy could see the wall through a vast cavity in the middle of the piano. "I feel partly responsible," she continued. "But you—" She pointed at Gordy. "You bear the blame equally as well."

"You're the one who attacked us," Gordy spat.

"We were provoked," she said. "We came with peaceful intentions and gave you ample opportunity to comply with our demands. Look at what we're armed with! Torpor Tonic and a few other mild concoctions. Had we wished ill toward you or your family, don't you think we would have equipped ourselves better? You had no reason to refuse us. Now, where is it?"

"Where's what?" Gordy asked.

She snapped her fingers. "Don't trifle with me, boy. Produce the Eternity Elixir or I shall be forced to take extreme measures. And what in the world is wrong with *you*?" Something behind Gordy had distracted Esmeralda, and she turned her attention away.

Max squinted in pain. Sweat dripped from his forehead, and he wailed in agony.

"Max? What happened to you?" Gordy asked.

Max's lips puckered, but he couldn't respond. Suddenly, he started to scream. Gordy cringed from the near-deafening sound. He wanted to cover his ears, but he couldn't move with the barbaric Burke clamping down on him.

"What did you do to him, Dieter?" Esmeralda asked the man gripping Max's arms.

"Nothing. I's just holdin' 'em," Dieter said in a gruff Scottish accent.

"Just holding him?" She scoffed. "The boy's all pale. I didn't tell you to do anything to anyone yet."

"You have to let him go! He needs medicine!" Gordy shouted as Max began to writhe. Had he broken something during the fall through the hole? What if Dieter had injected Max with some sort of violent potion? The results could be catastrophic!

Esmeralda narrowed her eyes. "Nonsense. I know a ruse when I see one. Let him wriggle all he wants, but don't you let go of him."

Dieter squeezed Max's arms and pulled him into a bear hug.

"Burke, search Gordy's pockets," she instructed. "I'm not waiting around any longer."

Burke hesitated. "But what if he has something in one of them? Something dangerous?"

"He'll let you know. Won't you, Gordy?"

Gordy wasn't listening to her. He couldn't peel his eyes off Max. His best friend looked on the verge of passing out. Profuse sweat glistened on Max's cheeks, and his lips had turned ashen.

"Well," Burke grunted. "There's nothing sharp, is there?" The man frisked Gordy, patting each leg cautiously, before slipping a finger into one of Gordy's pockets. He checked both the front and back ones, but then shook his head. "Ain't nothing here. At least not in his britches."

"Gordy?" Esmeralda's nose twitched. "I'm losing my patience."

Gordy's eyes flitted between Max and Esmeralda. "I don't have it." He pointed with his chin to the mass of vines on the ground. "Bolter does."

"Ah, I see." Kneeling, Esmeralda pulled a gleaming dagger from her leather satchel and cut away the vines from around Bolter's legs. "You stay still, sir, or I'll have to poke you," she warned.

Bolter lay rigid.

With the flat side of the dagger, she probed Bolter's pockets, her eyes widening when she discovered what she was looking for.

"There you are." She inserted the pointy end of the dagger into the pocket over Bolter's left hip.

Esmeralda eased her fingers into Bolter's pocket and had just extracted the Eternity Elixir when something whizzed by Gordy's ear and struck her squarely on the back. It happened so suddenly, Gordy hadn't seen from where the bottle had been thrown.

Esmeralda stiffened and spun around, brushing away the pieces of shattered glass and liquid from her shoulders. "Who threw that?" she demanded, glaring at Gordy.

Gordy looked around, desperately searching for who had come to the rescue. But there wasn't anyone else in the room.

Esmeralda looked up at the hole in the ceiling, brandishing the dagger in front of her. "Who's up there? Show yourself!" But no one appeared in the opening. She sniffed her jacket and gagged. "Did anyone see who threw it?"

"No, ma'am," Burke admitted. "I was watching the boy."

"Do ya hear that?" Dieter asked, the light from the room causing his silvery teeth to sparkle as he tilted his head to the side. "Is that not rain?"

Everyone stopped and mimicked Dieter. The fire in the stairwell still popped and crackled, but it had started to dwindle. Gordy could hear his heartbeat thudding in his ears as well as his own breathing. There was still the low drone of the smoke detectors, but beneath it all, there was something else. A rumbling from outside the house. It originated from afar and wasn't quite as loud as thunder, but the sound grew.

"It's not rain," Burke said boorishly. "Sounds kinda like . . ." He stopped as movement near the window forced the curtains to billow out.

A rat emerged from behind the curtain.

Esmeralda jammed her hand into her satchel, but she wasn't fast enough.

Another rat joined the first one. And then another. And then another. In mere moments, a hundred rats had scurried up the sidewalk and into the living room, pouring through the ruined front door and the immense holes in the windows.

Esmeralda dropped the Eternity Elixir. The vial of potion rolled a few feet away, but she didn't have time to collect it. The rats paid no attention to anyone else in the room. Only her. She tried to retreat, but tripped over Bolter's prostrate body, and slammed her rear end against the floor. Her eyes grew to the size of two ripe plums as she frantically rooted around in her bag for something to defend herself.

And still the rats came.

Gordy blinked, not believing what he was seeing. There were so many of them! Pink ones. Black ones. Dark gray ones with mangled whiskers and crooked tails. They snapped at each other, clambered over furniture, squeaking and chattering as they advanced.

Where had they all come from? Gordy had no idea there could be so many rodents in Ohio.

The first of the rats arrived at her shoes and climbed up her legs with their abrasive claws.

Esmeralda unleashed a bloodcurdling shriek. "Get them off me! Get them off me!"

Burke's hands slid from Gordy's arms, but the bearded man didn't seem to know what to do. The cigar dangled from his lips, and the tip lit a chunk of his whiskers on fire, but he paid no notice.

"Should . . . should I—" Burke scratched the side of his head. "I could . . . go get help!"

"Start grabbing them!" Esmeralda's screams transformed into gurgling sobs.

Were the rats eating her?

No, it appeared the rats were *nuzzling* her, even producing a purring sound like they were small, mangy cats. They clung to her arms and legs, their whiskers tickling Esmeralda affectionately. It was as though the rats were in love.

It finally dawned on Gordy what was going on. He spun around in time to see Max reach out with his hand and yank Dieter's ear as hard as he could.

Dieter squealed, but refused to let go of his prisoner, keeping his grip locked tightly around Max's arms, while Max wrenched wildly on the thug's ear a second time.

Something wasn't right, and both Gordy and Dieter realized it at the same time. How was Max able to hold on to Dieter's ear? That's when Gordy saw the third arm protruding from his best friend's side.

"What the devil?" Dieter released Max and backed away. "How is it you be pulling this off?"

Max held up all three of his hands and waved, a ridiculous grin spanning the width of his mouth.

Gordy immediately recognized his handiwork. "Extra Limb!" he shouted.

Of course! That was why Max had been in so much pain only moments before. At some point during the scuffle,

Max had uncorked one of Gordy's special potions and downed the contents.

"Which means . . ." Gordy pointed to Esmeralda, and Max nodded.

"Rat Magnet!" Max exclaimed.

With his hands still waving madly in the air, Max charged at Dieter.

Dieter wanted no part of the three-armed freak, and he turned on his heels and raced out of the room, his long, red hair whipping back and forth like a horse's tail.

"Oy! Where do you think you're going?" Burke called after Dieter.

Gordy didn't give him any time to wait for an answer. Diving to the ground, he knocked away a cluster of rats covering Esmeralda's arm and broke the satchel from her grasp.

"Hang on a sec, you lil' brat!" Burke shouted. It was the only thing he could say before Gordy sprayed him in the face with Esmeralda's bottle of Torpor Tonic and he crashed to the ground, stiff as a board.

"Well done, my prodigious friend!" Bolter exclaimed, once Gordy freed him from the Vintreet Trap. "You handled that exceptionally well."

Max cut away the spiderweb from Zelda and helped her to her feet.

"Agreed," Zelda said, eyeing the mass of rodents still clinging to Esmeralda as though she were their mother. "Did you come up with that all by yourself?"

Gordy shrugged. "Yeah, I guess." He located the Eternity Elixir vial next to a heap of debris on the floor and dropped it in his pocket.

Bolter clasped a hand on Gordy's shoulder. "Absolutely brilliant!"

"Hey! What about me?" Max raised his third hand. "I'm the one who drank this stuff. I don't even know if it will wear off."

"Don't worry. You should be back to normal in a couple of hours," Gordy said.

Max grinned. "Darn. I wanted to try out for the wrestling team next year. See if those punks could pin me down with this bad boy."

"Ahem." Someone cleared their throat, and Gordy turned to see a man and a woman dressed in bathrobes standing in the doorway. It was Mr. and Mrs. Judd, his elderly next-door neighbors. "Is everything all right?" Mr. Judd inquired, leaning forward on his cane.

"We heard some crashing and . . . screaming," Mrs. Judd added. She had an assortment of colored curlers lodged in her white hair.

"Oh my." Bolter fidgeted with the clasp of his satchel.

"What's that burning smell?" Mr. Judd squinted and stared at the ceiling.

"That, well, yes. What is that, exactly?" Bolter looked at Zelda for help.

"We were just having a campout in the living room," Gordy said. "That's all. We were telling stories and got kind of scared."

"Oh, Farley, they were just having a campout!" Mrs. Judd looked relieved. "Is that why your mother's in a sleeping bag?" She pointed to Esmeralda and the horde of nestling rats.

Bolter followed her finger. He opened his mouth, and then closed it, looking confused.

"They're not wearing their glasses," Gordy whispered to Bolter. "They're pretty much blind without them." He smiled at the Judds. "We were roasting marshmallows too.

In the fireplace. That's the burning smell. No big deal. We're sorry we woke you up."

Mr. Judd puffed out his cheeks. "I called 911. I thought there was a fire or a burglary or something."

It was at that moment Gordy heard sirens blaring in the distance. He knew it would happen eventually, but he still groaned in defeat. In a few minutes, the police would arrive, and the Stitser home looked like a war zone. Which might actually be a good thing because if the authorities knew about the rats, the crater in the ceiling, Gordy's dad swaddled in unexplained slime upstairs, and Max's additional appendage, they would probably deem his mom and dad as unfit parents.

"It's okay, dear." Mrs. Judd patted her husband's arm. "It's just a misunderstanding. Let's leave them to their campout. Maybe we could call the police before they get here and say we made a mistake."

"I don't know, Betty," Mr. Judd said. "I think I should look around first."

Mr. Judd had always been a tad sour. But who could blame him? The Stitsers weren't exactly outstanding neighbors. At least half a dozen exotic reptiles had wound up in the Judds' koi pond on more than one occasion.

"There's no need for that," Max said, rushing over to the doorway. "I'll walk you back to your house." He grabbed Mr. Judd's elbow with one hand and Mrs. Judds' elbow with the other. He then grabbed Mr. Judd's cane before it toppled over with his third hand.

"Aren't you the helpful sort," Mr. Judd said.

"We're quite all right." Mrs. Judd wriggled out of Max's grip. "We know our way home. You stay here with your family and enjoy the evening. Wait!" She jabbed her hand through the opening, preventing Max from shutting the door all the way behind them. "I almost forgot. Will you be coming over this weekend?" she asked. "We're having a get together, you know. Ruth Appleton is going to do a quilting demonstration, and Madge Tressle is bringing her world-famous brownies."

"Who on earth are you talking to, Betty?" Farley asked gruffly.

"Wanda, of course." Betty nodded back into the room. "We must have woken her up."

Gordy swallowed and looked at Bolter and Zelda. The three of them slowly turned around.

Esmeralda had risen to her feet. The rats dangled from her like an array of living ornaments, but she no longer wore a panicked expression. She flexed her arms, threw her head back, and swallowed a bottle of mystery potion.

All at once, the rodents stopped squirming as Esmeralda's body began to tremble. A few of the creatures dropped and scurried away, but the majority clung for dear life as the trembling escalated into ferocious spasms.

"Not good. Not good at all!" Bolter backed away. "Get to the garage. Quick!"

Gordy and Max didn't wait to be told twice. While

Esmeralda convulsed, the four of them raced out of the room.

Gordy smacked the button on the wall, and the garage door ascended. Max slid the van door open and climbed in; Gordy was right behind him. The ground began to vibrate. It felt like an earthquake. Gordy didn't know what Esmeralda was doing, but he knew he didn't want to wait around to see. In all the commotion, he hadn't noticed what became of the Judds. He could only hope the geriatric couple had gone home.

Zelda took the front passenger seat and pulled the belt across her lap. She held another lava bomb in her hand, poised to attack. Bolter was the last to enter the garage. He looked at the group seated in the Stitser family van, but paused in the doorway.

"Hurry up!" Gordy shouted. What was taking him so long? The ceiling was shaking. A multitude of his dad's tools and appliance parts dislodged from their holding spots along the perforated walls and toppled to the ground.

Bolter looked from the family van to the other car parked in the garage, wearing a bewildered expression. Suddenly, he started hopping up and down.

"Get out! Change cars!" he shouted, heaving open the Subaru's door and plopping in the front seat while laughing hysterically. "I completely forgot. Oh, this is a real treat!" Bolter gently caressed the steering wheel, his eyes darting around, taking in the various components of the dashboard. He glanced down at his watch, said something under his breath, and laughed again. "Yes! Everything should be calibrated perfectly!"

"What are you talking about?" Gordy asked, joining Max in the backseat. Zelda sat next to Bolter in the front. "This car doesn't work." The Subaru had been out of commission for quite some time.

"Doesn't work!" Bolter mocked. "My boy, it has never worked better." He bent down to look under the dash. "Now, it should be around here somewhere."

"Whatever you're looking for, I suggest you snap to it!" Zelda said. The tremors could be felt throughout the vehicle. How much longer would Esmeralda hold up?

"Ah, there you are." Bolter peeled a wedge of tape away from the gearshift and removed a miniscule vial of liquid, no bigger than a thimble. Tossing his head back, Bolter swallowed the potion, bottle and all. He smacked his lips with satisfaction.

Gordy slapped his forehead. "We don't have the keys! They're still in the kitchen."

Bolter clapped his hands together, and the car suddenly rumbled to life. The lights along the console turned on. He tapped the gas pedal with his foot, and the Subaru responded with a series of impressive growls.

"We need to get far, far away from here," Bolter said. But he wasn't speaking to the others; he had spoken to the car. With his nubby fingers steepled together beneath his chin, the gearshift moved into reverse.

"What's going on?" Max leaned forward in his seat,

then fell back again as the Subaru backed out of the garage all on its own.

"Fine work," Zelda said, impressed. "How does it heed your commands?"

Bolter tapped his temple with a stumpy knuckle. "Through my thoughts. I've been running trials on this particular compound for three years. Care to listen to some Golden Oldies?"

The radio magically turned on. The knob rotated until it located the desired station and an unfamiliar singer belted out a tune from the speakers.

Gordy grinned. "How long will the car stay under your control?" he asked.

"Long enough for us to put a healthy chunk of map between us and that woman," Bolter said.

The Subaru reached the edge of the driveway and rolled into the street. The brakes engaged, and the lever clicked as it shifted out of reverse. Gordy almost couldn't contain his excitement. Less than an hour ago, he had been cursing the moment of Bolter and Zelda's arrival. They were guilty of destroying almost everything in his home. But had they not arrived when they did, there was no way they could have escaped Esmeralda. It was a stroke of pure luck.

"Hang on to something!" Zelda shouted over the lively tune playing on the radio.

Gordy barely had time to turn his attention back to the house as the front wall suddenly exploded, and a massive blob of debris shot out from the hole like a cannonball.

No fewer than three dozen rats sprawled across the windshield of the Subaru, their beady, black eyes staring in at Gordy and the others. Glass, drywall, and the charred remains of a million dead insects rained down on the street. The Stitsers' home had been utterly demolished.

"We have to go back!" Gordy shouted above the sound of a barbershop quartet singing on the radio.

"Go back? Are you mad?" Bolter asked. The windshield wipers turned on, dispensing squeaking rodents to either side of the car.

"My dad!" Gordy gripped the headrest of Bolter's seat and leaned forward. "What's going to happen to him?"

"He's fine," Bolter said. "He's safer there than he would be with us right now, I assure you. My Tranquility Swathe will protect him from the elements, like I mentioned, and Esmeralda doesn't know where he's hiding."

"How do you know that?" Max asked.

"Because it appears she's in pursuit of us at the moment," Zelda said.

Gordy and Max looked through the back window as Esmeralda stepped through the enormous crater in the wall of the house. She held her hands at her sides as ropes of electricity coursed from her fingertips and traveled up and down her arms. Gordy would have loved to know what potion she had taken, but seeing the demented Elixirist standing in the middle of the street, her eyes glowing with white-hot light, squashed whatever questions he had.

"Where to now?" Zelda removed a small, tin cauldron from her bag and tossed in a handful of crumpled, dried leaves. She blew gently on the leaves and then tossed a pinch of strong-smelling pods into the mixture.

Mailboxes and fire hydrants whizzed by as the car zoomed down the road at blinding speed. Gordy could no longer see his house or Esmeralda, for that matter, through the rear window.

"I think we need an airport. We'll have to come up with some way to avoid security, though," Bolter said.

"What do you think I'm working on right now?" Zelda removed a metal flask from her satchel.

"Anaconda fangs," Max said, reading the scribbled writing on the label. "Shut up!"

She smiled. "I should be able to manage a camouflage within a few minutes."

There was a staticky crackle in the air. Though it seemed

to originate from inside the car, Gordy knew the sound came from somewhere else.

"You didn't really think you'd get away that quickly, did you?" Esmeralda's voice echoed in his ears.

Gordy balled his hands into fists as he looked for the woman. Somehow, Esmeralda had hijacked the use of Bolter's hearing pill, her voice coming through as loud and clear as if she were speaking into a microphone.

"The rat potion was an excellent touch. I'll give you bonus points for creativity. But I'm through playing games," she said.

Gordy stared at the others, who all wore concerned expressions.

"Mr. Bolter, you will arrive at B.R.E.W. Headquarters no later than two a.m. You will gain security clearance for me and four of my associates. You will then wait in the parking lot for thirty minutes. Then you will escort Gordy to the elevator where he will descend—alone—to the lowest level, bringing me the Eternity Elixir. Zelda and Max will head to level one where one of my associates will lock them in a holding cell. No tricks. No gimmicks."

She said it all so resolutely, no one in the car could muster an immediate response. It was Max who finally spoke up.

"Or what?" he asked. Gordy looked at him in confusion, and Max folded his arms across his chest. "She's got nothing, dude. We have the potion. We already kicked their butts. And now we're outta here. What does she have to bargain with?"

Gordy's phone vibrated in his pocket. He checked the screen and saw Adilene was on the line.

"Hey, Adilene, can I call you back?" Gordy asked, exasperated. "We're kind of in some serious trouble at the moment."

Adilene sighed. "Yeah, I know."

Gordy didn't like the sound of that. Something was wrong. "How do you know?" he asked.

"Yeltzin came through our wall. It was really cool until I realized what he was there for and then it wasn't really cool at all." Adilene still had a chip in her voice, but it was probably just for show.

Gordy dragged his fingers down his face in frustration. That was why he hadn't seen Yeltzin back at the house. The Russian had gone out to collect Adilene.

"Are you okay?" Gordy asked her, switching on the speaker of his phone so the others in the car could hear the conversation.

"Um, I am," she said. "But my parents are pretty upset!"

"They took all of you?" That was bad. Really bad. Esmeralda had stooped to a new low.

"Oh, Rivera!" Max growled.

"You're not hurt, are you?" Gordy asked.

"Don't worry about us, Gordy. We're fine. Although my mom has said at least a hundred times that I'm never allowed to hang out with you guys ever again. She just . . .

Yes, *sí, mamá*—" Gordy heard Mrs. Rivera's voice shouting at Abilene in Spanish. "My mother wants me to tell you that you will have to pay for all your *pupusas* from here on out."

"I'm sorry, Adilene. Tell your parents I'm sorry."

The line went dead. Gordy was at a loss of what to do. Despite having specific instructions from his mom to keep the Elixir out of Esmeralda's hands, he couldn't think of another solution. Gordy looked at Bolter through the rearview mirror, and Bolter nodded in understanding.

"I'm assuming you have devised a way past the protective wards," Bolter said, resuming the conversation with Esmeralda's disembodied voice. "I can gain access for all of you into the building, but it won't allow anyone in the Vessel room. That takes level-four clearance."

"Way to go, Bolter," Max muttered, shaking his head in disbelief. "Why don't you just tell her all our secrets?"

"Quiet down, Max," Zelda whispered gruffly. "Bolter's just looking out for Gordy's safety."

"Yes," Bolter said, nodding. "Without clearance past the Vessel's wards, Gordy faces perilous injuries."

"I will text you a recipe," Esmeralda said, her voice even. Calm. "See that you follow the instructions to the finite details, and don't waste a drop of the Elixir in fashioning that potion. Your friends don't have time to wait for it to self-replicate."

Bolter sighed and glanced sideways at Zelda. "She has thought of everything."

"Indeed I have," Esmeralda answered.

Bolter gave Esmeralda his number, and within seconds, his enormous, brick-shaped phone received the information. He handed the device to Zelda, who immediately rummaged in her satchel in search of the ingredients.

"You're lucky I carry black widow web and palomino horse whiskers in my case," Zelda said.

"What will the potion do?" Gordy asked.

"According to these instructions, it should give you the highest level of security clearance." Zelda shook her head. "I don't know how it's possible."

"The Eternity Elixir makes it possible," Bolter muttered. He raised his voice and addressed Esmeralda again. "What about the security guards? There are at least a dozen of them on duty. What will become of them?"

"I'll take care of security. You deliver Gordy and the Elixir on time. And if you raise any suspicions at B.R.E.W., I will vanish forever, along with Adilene and her parents."

Several moments of silence followed. Esmeralda had finished. She had offered up her terms and now it was Gordy's move.

Bolter and Zelda turned and faced the two boys in the backseat. The Subaru continued on its course. It engaged the turn signal and climbed the onramp of the freeway, heading in the direction of B.R.E.W. Headquarters.

"This is a dangerous game," Bolter warned.

"Agreed," Zelda said. "But what other options do we have?"

He puffed out his cheeks. "I see that we have two choices. One, we comply precisely with her commands. Gordy will deliver the Elixir to Esmeralda at the Vessel."

"But what will happen to Gordy when he does that?" Max asked, all at once serious.

"My guess is that nothing will happen to him or to the Rivera family. Esmeralda will have what she needs and will see no reason to keep them hostage any longer."

"Then what happens to you guys?" Gordy wondered.

"Yeah," Max chimed in. "What's on the first level?"

"Courtrooms, holding cells. All prisoners standing trial are processed there," Zelda explained. "Esmeralda said they'd lock us up. I assume we'll stay there until the employees show up for their morning shifts."

"We'll have to sleep in a jail cell?" Max started giggling. "That's not so bad."

"Once Esmeralda has the Elixir," Bolter continued, "it will take her a while to construct her desired potion. I'm assuming she has all the other necessary ingredients."

"What's the second choice?" Gordy asked.

Bolter gnawed on the inside of his cheek and gazed out the side window. "We do what we initially planned. We steer clear of B.R.E.W., board a plane, and leave the country."

"And abandon Adilene and her parents?" Gordy didn't consider that an option. "What do you think would happen to them if we did that?"

Zelda gave Bolter a sideways look. "It would be . . . unfortunate."

"Then we can't do it." Gordy shook his head. "Right?" He smacked Max's chest with the back of his hand.

"Yeah, probably not," Max grumbled.

"I understand your concern for your friend. It's very noble, my boy. But there's something you should know," Bolter said. "Should Esmeralda succeed in destroying the Vessel, there's a good chance that all of B.R.E.W.'s developments could cease. Permanently."

Gordy narrowed his eyes. "What does that mean?"

"We Elixirists have dabbled our fingers in almost every facet of society. Electricity. Medicine. Law enforcement. Plumbing. And the Vessel ties it all together. It melds the physical and the metaphysical into one. If the Vessel is destroyed, the world's technological advancements could revert back a hundred years or more. It would be like the Dark Ages."

"But we don't know that," Zelda said. "Do we?"

Bolter shrugged. "We've lived for three hundred years in a world where the Vessel has existed. Who knows what things will be like if it is gone? One thing's for sure, the Forbidden Zones would lift and all of the most dangerous Elixirists would walk free."

Gordy groaned. Why was this happening? It was all Aunt Priss's fault. Why hadn't she chosen somewhere else to send that package? There seemed to be nothing standing in the way of Esmeralda's plan. They had less than an hour to comply with her orders, which wasn't enough time to come up with anything else.

"Gordy, I'm sorry to say it, but this has to be your decision," Bolter said solemnly. "We can't decide for you. All that I ask is that you make your choice based on the greater good. Sacrifices must be made."

Gordy closed his eyes to think. What kind of world would it be if criminals suddenly broke out of their prisons and started running amok through the streets? But then Gordy thought about his friend Adilene and her parents. They were innocent players in this whole charade, and he had a chance to save them.

"Okay," he whispered, opening his eyes. "Let's head to B.R.E.W."

Bolter kept his hands on the wheel as the Subaru sped up the winding road towards the massive B.R.E.W. Headquarters. He wasn't steering, but he didn't want to raise any questions as they passed through the security checkpoints. The guard at the first outpost checked Bolter's and Zelda's badges. Bolter received a temporary pass for Max.

"I have a special companion with me today," Bolter said to the guard, his voice shaky and uneven. "And I have a few friends arriving later," he added. "This document should give them all the appropriate clearance." He handed the man a small piece of paper that Zelda had previously doused with the potion made from Esmeralda's recipe.

The guard perused the document, his forehead furrowing in confusion. "I'm not sure what this is," he said, his voice low and somewhat threatening.

Bolter swallowed. "Uh . . . you should be able to scan

it, I believe. Just there in your computer." He glanced nervously at Zelda. The green-haired Elixirist shrugged.

The guard studied Bolter for a moment, his one hand clutching the doctored paper, his other hand fingering the knob of his radio. Gordy held his breath, fearing the worst. If the guard spooked and called for reinforcements, no one would be allowed onto the premises. That meant horrible things would happen to Adilene.

After a grueling pause, the guard turned to his computer and ran the paper through a scanning device. An approving chirp sounded from the monitor, and after typing a few strokes on his keyboard, the man returned to the Subaru.

"Gordon Ethan Stitser, Junior," he said, ducking down to peer into the backseat. "Is that you?"

Gordy nodded and rolled down his window to accept the pass the guard handed him. The words printed on the upper right-hand corner of the badge announced his level-four clearance.

Bolter waved at the guard as they drove past. "That went surprisingly smooth," he said.

"Yes, unfortunately," Zelda added. "I had hoped that a Tainted document would've set off the highest alarm."

Gordy didn't say anything. He understood why Zelda felt that way. They were about to hand over a deadly weapon to a horrible dark Elixirist, who would then have the power to destroy B.R.E.W., the Vessel, and everything good his mom had worked for. The world would change for the worst, but at the moment, all Gordy wanted to do was save Adilene and her folks. That was all that mattered.

"Your mom works here?" Max asked as they approached the south entrance of the building. He stared up at the high walls, bewildered. "It's that kooky cream and oil place, Somnium."

"I know," Gordy said. "I told you that." He strained his ears to hear Zelda and Bolter, who were whispering to each other in the front seat.

"Yeah, but, I didn't really think B.R.E.W. was inside that building," Max said. "Oh, man!" Max whined, gawking down at his side. Gordy watched as Max's third arm began to fizzle rapidly. Fortunately, Max didn't show any signs of pain from the change, though he twitched and spasmed a bit. Max groaned and giggled and flapped his extra limb like a wing until it dissolved completely, leaving only a hole in his shirt where the arm had burst free.

Bolter pulled into a parking stall and turned off the engine. The Subaru whined and hissed, and the radio died. Gordy turned in his seat and watched as a pair of headlights attached to a white SUV approached the front security gate. Another car followed closely behind it. More of Esmeralda's thugs, Gordy assumed. The vehicles proceeded without incident, pausing only briefly at each security post before heading to the south end of the building and vanishing from sight.

Gordy checked the time on the dashboard clock: 3:10. Twenty minutes until showtime. He felt his stomach tighten. What was he going to do? How could he stop Esmeralda from carrying out her plan? He may have been a skilled Dram, even a borderline Elixirist, but in this situation, Gordy felt like the most incompetent person alive. If only they had managed to completely subdue Esmeralda back at the house. Prevented her from moving, somehow. Gordy slumped in his seat. He should have at least kept eyes on that crafty Russian and stopped him from stealing off to the Riveras' house.

"Why not Blotch us?" Zelda hissed at Bolter under her breath. "Why go to all this trouble, then risk the chance that we try to stop her? Which we fully intend to do." Zelda's brow furrowed, and she kept checking the contents of her satchel, ensuring she had some sort of weapon to protect her. "Had she expertly Blotched us, we could've entered B.R.E.W. months ago and carried out her plan. We'd be none the wiser until we awoke in shackles."

"Who are we to Esmeralda?" Bolter fired back. "She had no idea of our involvement until tonight. Besides, she needed the Elixir first. I suspect had Priscilla sent her delivery to one of us instead of the Stitsers, we'd be having an entirely different conversation right now."

"Why not Blotch the boy then?" Zelda asked.

"She tried," Gordy said. Bolter and Zelda glanced over their shoulders. "When she came to my house the first night, she Blotched my dad instead with her business card."

"But not you?" Zelda peered back, a brightly painted eyebrow raised inquisitively.

"That's because she underestimated Gordy Stitser," Bolter said, giving Gordy a wink. "How could a child cause so much trouble?"

"Well, she won't be making that mistake again. Here we go." Zelda nodded at the clock. "Time to move."

The four of them exited the car and headed for the south entrance of the building. After dropping Zelda and Max off on the first level, Bolter accompanied Gordy through the building to the elevator. He didn't say much. Once or twice, Bolter attempted to give Gordy some sort of instruction on how to thwart Esmeralda, but each time he shook it away, dismissing it with a wave of his nubbed hands. It was too dangerous. Not worth risking Gordy's life or the lives of the Riveras.

"It will be all right, Gordy," Bolter insisted. "This is just a hiccup. B.R.E.W. will bounce back and we will increase our security. Criminals like Esmeralda have singularly-tracked minds. She plays the game one move at a time and that will be her downfall."

"But if she destroys the Vessel," Gordy said, "we won't have a way to counter any of her moves."

Bolter's nostrils flared. "Indeed. Well, there's nothing to do with it now. Patience, my friend." He patted Gordy on the shoulder. "And this is as far as I go."

As the elevator doors closed, Gordy felt the floor drop downward and an uncomfortable pit formed in his stomach. This was it. He was alone now and with nothing other than the Eternity Elixir in his pocket. No potions or ingredients to whip something up in a pinch. The elevator stopped and the doors opened.

"Hello, friend." Yeltzin pulled Gordy by his arm out of the elevator and then sprang into the empty space, checking all four corners. "That's a good boy," he said, once he had ensured the room was secure. "You brought present, no?"

"No . . . I mean, yes," Gordy answered. He crammed his hand into his pocket, but Yeltzin stopped him.

"No, no. You bring the Elixir to her. It will mean more." He motioned for Gordy to hold up his hands and then he did a quick pat down, frisking him for any weapons.

"Where's Adilene?" Gordy demanded. "Where are her parents?"

"Shush." Yeltzin held his finger up to his lips. Then he pointed down to where the glow from the Vessel poured through the glass window, lighting up the end of the hallway.

"Gordy Stitser, welcome!" Esmeralda clapped her hands together. She stood at the back of the room along with a couple of other people, all of whom wore coats and had beards. Apparently, no one in Esmeralda's company ever shaved.

The Vessel rested upon its crystal pedestal, the silvery liquid roiling within the cup. Esmeralda had constructed a mini-lab beside it, consisting of two Bunsen burners heating a limestone cauldron. A collection of exotic ingredients was lined up along the bench. Gordy recognized a few of them instantly. He saw scorpion stingers and a jar of cobra

hoods swimming in some sort of pickling solution. Gordy also noticed what looked like an egg with red veins.

Esmeralda saw him eyeing the assortment. She pointed to the egg. "It's an Epizootic Egg. The Mapuche Shamans from Chile use them to capture diseases from the sick. Very rare and highly toxic."

"All of that stuff is," Gordy said. Other than the scorpion stingers, most of the items on the bench were illegal throughout the potion community.

"You're right. The potion I intend to make requires such ingredients. But the most important will be that one in your pocket. Yes, Gordy, you may show it to me now."

Esmeralda's two companions moved away from her to stand behind Gordy, blocking his escape.

Gordy started to reach for the Elixir, but stopped. "Where are my friends?"

"They are safe," Esmeralda said. "Once we make the potion and pour it into the Vessel, you'll be free to leave with them."

"I want to see them now or I won't give it to you!"

She rolled her eyes. "You do realize you don't have much wiggle room here, don't you?" She turned to Yeltzin. "Bring them to me."

The Russian left the room, and a few minutes later, Adilene and her parents appeared in the hallway, looking through the glass pane at Gordy.

Adilene half smiled. Both she and her parents were bound in a thick rope. They looked to be all right, though

Mr. and Mrs. Rivera could have melted the glass with the angry lasers shooting from their eyes.

"Now, Gordy, this particular draught requires dual mixing. Do you know what that means?" Esmeralda sounded almost like a teacher giving instructions. If Gordy hadn't known her words to be laced with venom, he would've thought she seemed rather pleasant.

"It means you need someone else to help you put in the ingredients," Gordy answered.

"Very good." She batted her eyelashes at Gordy.

"What, me?" he blurted. "I'm not helping you make that! Get one of your goons to do it."

She frowned. "I would, but I need my 'goons' to guard the entrance and make sure your friends stay put. And, to be honest, I need someone with a deft hand. Someone I can trust to perform everything flawlessly."

Gordy scoffed. "I'll mess it up on purpose."

"Would you?" Esmeralda gestured to the window. "If your friend's life depended on it, would you be so careless?"

On cue, Yeltzin moved behind Adilene and placed his hands on her shoulders.

Gordy tensed, his anger boiling up inside of him. "Get your hands off her!"

"We're typically not the violent sort, I hope you understand that. However, we have grown desperate. Do you love your parents? Of course you do," Esmeralda answered for him. "And so do I. But I haven't seen my parents in quite some time, and I miss them immensely. I need this potion to work in order to have a reunion with them. If that requires a little blood on my hands, so be it. But it doesn't have to be that way."

"What do you want me to do?" Gordy lowered his eyes to the cauldron.

"Simple. I'll perform all the ceremonial pieces. You just have to add the proper dosages on my cues. No mistakes though, or you'll force my hand, or rather Yeltzin's hand. Understood?"

Esmeralda increased the heat on the burners, the left side hotter than the right. She snapped her fingers and sprinkled dried poison oak into the mixture. After waiting a few moments, she nodded to Gordy.

"The jellyfish tentacles, all of them, but one by one from the container," she instructed.

Gordy obeyed, and after the third tentacle dropped into the cauldron, the potion changed from yellow to a pale pink.

Esmeralda reduced the heat on both burners and added several cobra hoods, whispering something to each one as they fell. She snipped the barbs from the nightshade stems with a pair of copper shears and then stirred the potion with one of the scorpion stingers. It was the most elaborate brewing Gordy had ever witnessed. So many steps. So many dangerous ingredients. He was told to pour in a vial of sea snake venom and then, while she sprinkled in more poisonous herbs, he inserted the tip of a rusty railroad spike into the center of the cauldron. Gordy bit his lip in concentration, partly because he feared what would happen once they arrived at the conclusion and partly because of the complicated procedure.

Finally, Esmeralda picked up the Epizootic Egg and held it high above her head. She began to chant as she lowered the egg and cracked the shell with her thumbs. Ooze dripped out followed by a sickening black yolk.

The potion began to bubble, the cauldron rattling against the burners.

"Gordy," Esmeralda whispered. "Uncork the Eternity Elixir and, on my mark, pour it in." As if sensing Gordy's possible defiance, she shot him a warning glare. "Don't do anything stupid. Think about your friends."

Gordy's chest ached, and he looked one final time at the window.

Adilene stood there, staring back at him, Yeltzin's imposing frame towering over her and her parents.

"I'm sorry," Gordy mouthed to her.

Then Adilene winked.

Gordy paused in confusion. Was it a twitch? A nervous impulse? No, it had been a distinct gesture. Adilene had winked as though she was trying to tell him something.

Suddenly, Adilene shook away Yeltzin's massive hands from her shoulders and spun around. The Russian glared at her, but as he reached for her, Adilene hauled off and kicked him sharply on the knee. Yeltzin yelled out in surprise, and then something struck him on his chin and shattered. A cloud of gas enveloped his bewildered face as he collapsed, vanishing from the window. Gordy watched in amazement as Adilene appeared to kick the giant Russian once again while he lay on the floor. Then before she could explain what was happening, she wriggled out of the rope binding her, grabbed her parents by the arm, and raced away from the room.

Esmeralda looked at the window in confusion. "What is this?" she demanded. "Caldwell. Drummond! Go find out what's going on."

It was then that both Gordy and Esmeralda realized her other two henchmen were missing from the room as well.

But there *was* somebody else there.

Wanda Stitser stepped from the shadows, a vial of potion clasped in her hand.

"Mom?" Gordy gasped.

Esmeralda didn't hesitate. She plunged her hand into her satchel and then into the bubbling cauldron. Before Wanda could toss her weapon, Esmeralda slipped behind Gordy and held something at his throat.

Gordy felt the tip of a needle grazing his skin. Esmeralda had filled a syringe with the poisonous potion.

"Don't!" Wanda held up her hand.

"Drop it!" Esmeralda ordered. "Whatever it is you're holding, I want to see it on the floor in three, two . . ." She shook the syringe, and Gordy's mom immediately knelt and set the vial on the ground. "Very good. Hello, Wanda. We've never formally been introduced. My name is—"

"I know who you are," Wanda interrupted.

"You're not alone, are you?"

Wanda shook her head. "My sister, Priscilla, took out the rest of your thugs, with Adilene's help, of course." She nodded at Gordy. "That girl's got spunk. I like her."

Gordy didn't know what to say. He had no idea Adilene could be so aggressive.

"I'm impressed," Esmeralda said. "Did you have a pleasant stay in Greenland?"

"Quite."

Gordy could feel the tip of the syringe trembling and could sense Esmeralda's trepidation. She was terrified. *Good!* Gordy thought. *Let's see how she likes squaring off with one of the greatest Elixirists in the world.*

"Now, let my son go," his mom said.

Esmeralda clicked her tongue. "Oh, I don't think so. I need him to finish what we started."

Gordy glanced down at the Eternity Elixir still in his fingers. The cork had been removed, and the pearly liquid shimmered in the vial.

"You're not leaving this place tonight," Mrs. Stitser said.

"Of course I am. Once we complete my potion and drop it into the Vessel, you'll have no power over me. No ability to brew or concoct a weapon. Ah, you knew this, didn't you?" she asked.

Gordy stared at his mom, unsure of what Esmeralda meant.

"It makes no difference to me," Gordy's mom said. "With or without my abilities, I will still put a stop to you."

"What's she talking about, Mom?" Gordy asked.

Esmeralda chuckled. "Oh, my dear, Gordy. Soon, very soon, you shall be the only Elixirist in your family. But that won't last long if your mother tries to prevent my escape. I'll end his life, Wanda, and I won't lose any sleep over it."

Gordy watched his mom. He could see her softening. There was nothing she could do from across the room. If she tried to throw anything at Esmeralda, the woman would jab Gordy with the needle. Everything about that wicked potion screamed of death: the jellyfish, the stingers, the weird egg. One drop of that potion in Gordy's veins and it would be all over.

"We were just about to conclude," Esmeralda continued. "Why don't you take a seat and watch? I'd be interested to know any sensations you feel as your abilities are swept away."

"The destruction of the Vessel will only affect a select few of B.R.E.W.," Wanda said, lowering herself to the ground. "The others will come after you for what you've done. They won't stop until they've captured you."

"Yes, but I'll be long gone by then, and I'll have company." She squeezed Gordy's arm. "Gordy, if you don't mind, it's time to pour in the Elixir."

Gordy looked down once more at the vial. There really wasn't much to it. A simple glass container and some liquid.

He had no idea how it could do all the things Bolter said it could do. Gordy rolled the vial between his fingers, making the potion swirl. Could the Elixir do anything by itself?

Gordy glanced up at his mom. "I'm sorry." His voice caught in his throat.

"It's not your fault, dear," she said. "I'm so proud of how brave you've been. You know how I said you would become a great Elixirist one day? Well, I was wrong. You're already there."

"But I don't want you to lose your powers."

His mom smiled warmly. "It won't be all that bad. Maybe you could teach me again. That would be fun. And besides, it will give me more to talk with your father about."

"Come on, boy." Esmeralda forced Gordy to face the cauldron. "Hurry up!"

Gordy's shoulders slumped. He took a deep breath, lifted the Eternity Elixir, and poured the potion directly into his mouth.

The next few moments passed by in a blurry haze. Gordy heard screams from both Esmeralda and his mother. He felt the sting of the needle at his throat, but then it fell away as his mom launched a gleaming, golden potion across the room. It hurtled end over end, and Gordy watched it tumble as if it was traveling in slow motion. There were so many sounds. The clatter and splashing of the overturned cauldron. The hissing of noxious steam rising in the air. And through it all, Esmeralda never stopped screaming. Then he blacked out.

When Gordy woke up, he was in a bed. But not his bed. His bed had a fluffy down comforter and an X-Men movie poster above the headboard. Still, the bed felt warm and safe. He blinked his eyes several times and stretched.

"Hello," a soft voice said next to his ear.

"Ah!" Gordy belted out in surprise. "You're not my mom!"

"No, I am not," the man answered. He was wearing

scrubs and a pair of wiry glasses that rested halfway down the bridge of his nose. He looked like a doctor, but something told Gordy that he wasn't a regular doctor. The man pressed the end of a stethoscope to Gordy's chest and listened to his heartbeat.

"Who are you?" Gordy asked.

"The name's Parley. And I'm not a doctor."

"I didn't think so."

"However, I do study Dire Substances for a living. Like the one you ingested two days ago."

"Two days ago!" Gordy sat straight up. "I've been sleeping for two days?"

"Yes." Parley removed the earbuds of his stethoscope. "From what I can tell, you seem to be faring better now."

"What does that mean?" Gordy asked.

"I don't know," Parley said with a halfhearted shrug. "Could mean the effects of the strange potion you drank had no lasting impact on your insides. Bizarre as that would seem."

The door to the room suddenly burst open, and Gordy's mom and dad appeared.

"Oh, thank heavens!" His mom closed her eyes and pressed her hand against her chest.

"Hey," Gordy said, his voice shaky and unstable. Both parents looked on the verge of tears, and Gordy was about to join them. Gordy's mom threw her arms around his shoulders and hugged him tighter than he had ever been hugged.

"Hey, Gordo," his dad said. "How are you feeling?"

Gordy was glad to know his dad was safe. The last time he had seen him, his dad had been mummified in Bolter's Tranquility Swathe.

"Fine, I guess." Other than disoriented, Gordy felt good, actually. Maybe the Eternity Elixir did that to you when you drank it. "What happened?"

"We almost lost you. Several times." His mom looked at Parley. "How are his vitals?"

"Yeah, is he showing any side effects?" his dad asked.

"Everything seems shipshape," Parley answered. "Excellent blood pressure. Normal temperature. Breathing is regular, though he does snore." He winked at Gordy.

"That was an incredibly stupid thing you did," Mrs. Stitser said to Gordy. "You're lucky to be alive. I don't ever want to go through something like that again."

"I didn't know what else to do," Gordy said in his defense.

"You were to do exactly as you were told. Trying to be a hero was not the instruction."

Gordy stared at the sheets, not wanting to make eye contact with his mom's intense gaze. He'd definitely put her through a lot. "I'm sorry, Mom."

His dad reached over and squeezed Gordy's foot. "You were very brave, and you dealt with more than a normal twelve-year-old would ever have to deal with."

"Yes, that's true," she agreed with a sigh. "If it wasn't for you, Gordy, we would be in worse shape."

Gordy glanced up at them and smiled weakly.

"But, I'm afraid we're going to have to ground you," his dad said.

"Ground me?" Gordy asked, but then nodded, not surprised. "I guess I knew that might be coming."

"Yep, you can no longer go down to your mom's lab ever again."

"Are you serious?" Gordy's eyes widened. That seemed extreme even considering all the trouble Gordy had caused.

"Have you seen our house lately?" Gordy's mom asked, smiling. "The whole thing burned down. There's no lab left. I suppose we can make an exception for the lab we build in our next home. Whenever that happens."

Gordy exhaled and slumped against the headboard. His dad whispered something to Mrs. Stitser and she nodded.

"I'll be there shortly," she answered.

Mr. Stitser turned to Gordy. "I have to go, pal. I have a meeting with our insurance company. They want details about the gas leak explosion. At least that's what we're calling it. There had to be some sort of gas used in the attack on our house, right?"

Gordy grinned sheepishly at his mom. "That was definitely not my fault," he said. "You're the one who sent Bolter and Zelda to help."

She sucked back on her teeth. "I guess I did set us up for disaster. Hopefully the insurance company will cover some of the damages. But we're going to have to move, unfortunately. We'll stay with Grandma and Grandpa Stitser for a while."

Gordy's dad leaned forward and kissed Gordy on the top of his head. "I love you, Gordo," he said. "I'll be back in a few hours." He said good-bye to Gordy's mom and to Parley and then exited quietly out the door.

"What is this place?" Gordy asked, staring around the room.

"This is my home," Parley said. "I'm Parley, remember. We just met." He held out his hand and Gordy shook it. "I'll leave you two alone. If you need anything at all, I'll be downstairs." He excused himself from the room.

Gordy's mom glanced at her fingers. "Parley's a very skilled Philter—someone who can remove ingredients and potions from inside you. There are only a handful in the world, and he's the resident Bio-Philter at B.R.E.W. Headquarters. The Elixir shut down your body completely. Normally, we would have given you something to counteract the potion you drank, but there was no way to make an antidote to help it work its way out of your system or even stabilize you while it remained. The Eternity Elixir was different from anything we've ever dealt with. Even after the glass vial refilled with the liquid, we could detect trace amounts still in your bloodstream. So we had to remove the dangerous ingredients from inside you." She paused to collect her emotions. Her jaw clenched, her voice trembling. "We had to work fast and without making any mistakes. We were fortunate the best Philter in the country happened to live so close by."

"Who's 'we'?" Gordy asked.

"Everyone. We've all been here for the past two days, watching over you. Your father, Bolter, and Zelda . . ."

"And let's not forget me, Mrs. Stitser." Max poked his head through the doorway.

"Hey, Max," Gordy said, relieved to see his boisterous friend.

Gordy's mom smiled and nodded. "I have to admit, Max definitely impressed me with how concerned he was for your well-being."

"I practically held your hand the entire time," Max added.

Though he looked a little tired, Max appeared to be alright, as did Adilene. She was standing behind Max as if debating whether or not she should join them.

"Why are you hanging out in the hallway?" Gordy asked her, motioning for Adilene to join them.

Adilene stared at her shoes, but slid into the room.

"She thinks everyone's still mad at her for getting kidnapped by Esmeralda," Max said.

"I do not!" Adilene protested.

"Yes, you do." Max rolled his eyes. He cupped his hand around his mouth and leaned close to Gordy. "And for good reason too."

"Now, now, Max," Gordy's mom said. "Adilene did a pretty good job taking down Yeltzin all by herself."

Gordy remembered Adilene fighting Yeltzin just before his mom appeared in the Vessel room. "Yeah, what happened? One second you were being held hostage, the next you were standing over the Russian, kicking him."

Adilene grinned. "I can't take all the credit for that. Your Aunt Priscilla told me what to do, and then she took care of the rest."

"My Vintreet Trap could've never dropped someone as big as Yeltzin without some help." Aunt Priss stood in the doorway, leaning against the jamb. "And Adilene was brave enough to heed my instruction without any hesitation. You have great friends, Gordy. Loyal and strong. The best kind there is." Aunt Priss looked just how Gordy remembered her, a slightly younger and wilier version of his mother. She had auburn hair and wore a long black sweater that ended just above her knees. "Hey, buddy." Her eyes glistened as she looked at Gordy.

"Your Aunt Priss showed me a shrunken head!" Max said with a cheerful grin.

"She did?" Gordy asked.

"It was awesome!" Max rubbed his hands together. "I threw up a little."

"Max, don't we need to be somewhere right now?" Adilene prodded Max in the ribs.

"I don't have anywhere to go," Max said with a shrug.

"You're seriously impossible!" Adilene grabbed Max's sleeve and tugged him toward the door.

Once they were out of the room, Aunt Priss moved

slowly to the side of the bed. She looked at Gordy's mom for a brief moment and then timidly rested her hands on Gordy's pillow. "You're mad at me, aren't you?"

Gordy opened his mouth to answer her, but then closed it abruptly. Was he mad at her? He didn't know the story behind her decision to send the Eternity Elixir to his home, but it had to be due to circumstances beyond her control. The Aunt Priss he knew wouldn't want any harm to come to him or his family.

Gordy shook his head. "No, I'm not mad. But you owe me."

She smiled and tousled his hair. "Big time. Do you want a shrunken head as well?"

"Two shrunken heads." Gordy held up his fingers.

"Two?" She laughed, and then narrowed her eyes. "What about Max's shrunken head?"

Gordy snorted. "No way! That's as small as his head could ever get."

Everyone was safe: Gordy's family, his best friends, and his two new Elixirist friends Bolter and Zelda. He couldn't have asked for a better result. Yes, his family would have to move and start over, but seeing his mom standing beside the bed smiling down at him made everything just fine.

"What happened to Esmeralda?" Gordy asked.

"She's been banished," his mom answered.

"Really?" Gordy nibbled on the inside of his cheek. "You banished her? Where?"

Wanda frowned. "It wouldn't be safe to tell you, but

rest assured she is far from here and will not be doing any more damage to our home any time soon."

"There were others too. Yeltzin and those other creeps." Gordy recalled being held captive by Dieter and Burke in their living room. "What happened to them?"

Gordy's mom exchanged a tired look with Aunt Priss. "They're on the move, but B.R.E.W. should be rounding them up soon enough."

"Don't worry about them, Gordy," Aunt Priss said. "They were just Esmeralda's hired help. Without her at the helm, they'll want no part of B.R.E.W. or any of the Stitsers for that matter. I can't stop thinking about what could've happened had you not been so levelheaded, Gordy."

"Or had you not shown up when you did," Gordy added. "That was lucky."

"It was close," his mom agreed. "But it was more than luck. We had a little help."

"From who?"

Wanda looked at Priscilla as she pulled out the familiar glass vial containing the Eternity Elixir. "I made a promise, Gordy, one I suppose I should keep. And I'd like to take you on a trip with me, as soon as you're up for it."

Gordy leaned forward, resting his hands on his legs. "A trip where?"

"I think it's time for you to meet your Grandpa Rook."

A re you nervous?" Gordy's mom asked, coming to an abrupt halt beyond the narrow entryway into the cavern. They had been walking for quite some time, and Gordy's feet ached. Both of them wore warm parkas and heavy waterproof boots with laces ending just below their knees.

Gordy glanced behind him, noticing the two rows of deep footprints in an otherwise seamless white landscape.

"A little, yeah," he said. There was no point in denying his fear. The whole atmosphere of the location screamed creepy. It started with the barbwire fence guarding the mountain range. His mom had passed him a pair of glasses to decode the words posted on the sign.

BE WARNED!
This is the Forbidden Zone of Mezzarix,
Scourge of Nations.

That didn't seem too inviting.

"What does 'Scourge of Nations' mean?" Gordy had asked her.

"It means he wasn't very popular among the civilized," she had answered.

Then there was the eerie blanket of snow covering everything. Gordy counted exactly three birds as they walked. Only three! He saw nothing else living. And now they were about to enter a crack in the mountain, headed for his grandfather's cave. A grandfather who had once tried to overthrow B.R.E.W.

"Are *you* nervous?" Gordy asked.

His mom took a breath and held it. She stared into the cavern, twitching her nose back and forth as she contemplated the question. Slowly, she exhaled. "No. It will be just fine. Dad's not a . . . horrible man." She removed one of her gloves and blew into her cupped hand. "He was always kind to Priss and me. Family means a lot to him."

"Then why did he do all those things?" Gordy asked.

"In his mind, he believed he was doing right." She squeezed Gordy's arm. "But he was wrong, Gordy. So very wrong. No matter what he tells you in there, remember that. He can be convincing when he wants to and that could be dangerous. You don't want to let him influence you in any way."

"He won't, Mom." Gordy nodded reassuringly. "I don't even know the guy and I probably won't like him."

His mom smiled, but her eyes revealed sadness. "I wish that were the case, dear."

The first thing Gordy noticed about his grandfather as he stood in the mouth of the cave was his hair. There was so much of it that it seemed to flow out like the mane of a white lion. He was dirty and old, wrinkly and skinny. He wore a tuxedo, at least that's what Gordy thought it looked like, and he was barefoot. In a word, Gordy initially thought his Grandpa Rook looked evil. But as they drew closer, and Gordy received a better look at his face, he noticed his grandfather's eyes. They seemed kind, thoughtful, and maybe even a little timid.

Grandpa Rook moistened his lips and clasped his hands together. "Well, hello, Gordy. How do you do?"

Gordy glanced at his mom for confirmation, and she encouraged him with a reassuring nod.

"I'm okay," he said. "How are you?"

Grandpa Rook narrowed his eyes. "Freezing. Should we gather around the fire? I've prepared a meal." He held up his hand. "No worries, Wanda. This particular batch of gruel won't be tainted."

The inside of the cave was simple, a few pieces of furniture, chairs, a bed, a bookcase or two. A warm fire burned in the center of the room, heating a black pot. Gordy could smell potatoes and savory herbs and started to feel a hint of hunger. They had a good meal on the flight, but their hike up the mountain had only allowed for trail mix and fruit.

"No Caribou Moss?" his mom asked, pointing to the pot. "Where did you get all that?"

"This is a special occasion, so I pulled out all the stops," Mezzarix said.

———

After dinner, Grandpa Rook requested to speak with Gordy alone. To Gordy's surprise, his mother didn't object.

"So tell me what you know," he said to Gordy once they were seated next to each other around the fire.

"About you?" Gordy asked. "That you died in a farming accident in Idaho before I was born. At least, that's what Mom told me until recently. Now, I guess I heard you were a very powerful Elixirist who kind of went crazy."

Mezzarix twiddled his thumbs and stared at the cavern floor. "Kind of, I suppose."

This felt awkward. What were they supposed to talk about? Gordy couldn't help but look at his grandfather's bare feet. They had to be freezing.

"Don't you have socks or boots or something?"

"Unfortunately, no. I can't wear them. The banishment terms won't allow it. That's how they keep me here."

"Oh." Gordy wanted to ask more about the whole banishment thing, but he wasn't sure how or where to start.

"It's not so bad, though." His grandpa lifted his feet and wiggled his toes. "I apply a warming balm to my soles every morning. It keeps out most of the cold."

Gordy raised his eyebrows. "Cool . . . I mean, that's awesome. So you're still allowed to make stuff while you're banished?"

He grinned bashfully. "Well, no, technically I shouldn't even have ingredients. But a true Elixirist will always find a way, you know? Speaking of which, your mother has told me quite a deal about you and your abilities. Care to share with an old man?"

Gordy nodded enthusiastically. "What do you want to know?"

The two of them spent the next hour testing Gordy's Deciphering abilities on several of Mezzarix's personal potions. Gordy recognized every ingredient in every vial, just by means of his nose. The old man was noticeably impressed. Mezzarix tried Philtering next, or the art of removing potentially hazardous ingredients from concoctions and rendering them harmless. Gordy displayed equal skill in that as well. Then came time to Blind Batch.

"I don't know what that means," Gordy said.

"Simply put, it is the art of mixing potions blindly, without a menu or prior direction," his grandpa said. "Have you ever just known what to add to a mixture?"

Gordy thought back to when he made the ice ball to stop Bawdry. He had just *known* what would work and what wouldn't. And it hadn't been his first time doing that either. In fact, he had made many potions without any knowledge beforehand of what to do.

His grandfather seemed to understand Gordy's expression and nodded. "Blind Batching is a rare talent. You could go your whole life and never meet anyone with such a gift."

"Can you do it?" Gordy asked.

"I can. And it would appear the skill has passed onto you. What should we make, Gordy?" Mezzarix held out his hand toward the cauldron. "I have some ingredients at my disposal. What would you want to create?"

"I don't understand. It doesn't work that way with me." Maybe Gordy really couldn't Blind Batch. Maybe his grandfather was mistaken. "I don't think of what I want to do and then just do it. It's different."

"How's it different?"

"Well, it's kind of like I start with an empty cauldron, and then I add an ingredient. After I do that, I add another one. And then another. And then something tells me to turn down the heat, or stir it differently." It was difficult to explain, but that was how it worked.

"It's the same with me, only I've come to realize how to control it. The mind builds based on necessity. So whether you understand it or not, your brain has already decided what you need before you start. Trust me when I tell you this, there are no limits for you, Gordy Stitser."

The two of them whispered back and forth. They told jokes, Gordy frequently laughed, and his grandfather even managed to sneak in a proud, gentle clap on his grandson's back from time to time. It was as though the two of them had known each other for all Gordy's life and were finally having a grand reunion.

When Wanda reappeared in the cave, clutching the Eternity Elixir, only then did they cease their jovial discussion.

"It's time," she said.

"You should stay longer. I could make up a couple of beds, something more comfortable. You could leave in the morning," Mezzarix suggested.

Gordy's mom shook her head. "I've made travel arrangements already. I need to get my son home and back to a normal life."

Mezzarix looked on the verge of protesting, but he gave a sideways glance to Gordy and closed his mouth. "Okay. Bring me the Elixir."

Gordy watched his mother cross the room. She hesitated a moment before handing the vial over to her father.

"Relax, dear," Mezzarix said soothingly. "I'll keep my end of the bargain. You know I will."

The ceremony wasn't as complicated as the one Esmeralda performed at B.R.E.W., but it was remarkable to watch. Seeing his grandfather concoct was witnessing a master at work. Using only the ingredients at his table, Grandpa Rook created a mixture into which he added several drops of his blood.

"That's how this all started," he explained to the two of them. "Because of my blood connection, I'm the only one who could have ever destroyed it." He gave Gordy's mom an awkward grin. "But you already knew that, didn't you?"

She held his gaze for a moment and then nodded. "I had my suspicions. But I didn't dare bring you the vial because I knew you would never destroy it."

"Until now," Mezzarix said, giving Gordy a quick wink before returning his attention to the potion.

He finalized the ceremony by pouring every ounce of the Eternity Elixir into his cauldron. The potion produced a soft hissing sound as the steam drifted toward the ceiling.

"It's done," Mezzarix said.

"That's it?" Gordy asked, somewhat put out by how quietly the potion had ended. It had caused a great deal of turmoil and to suddenly be over without so much as a mini-explosion was depressing.

"That's it." Grandpa Rook's nostrils flared. "My greatest creation is no more."

"Really?" Gordy looked at his mom for proof.

"I apologize if I don't trust you, Dad," Wanda said. She held out her hand for the empty vial. "I'll take that with me just to be sure."

"You won't need to, but if that's what you wish." He gave her the bottle.

"Regardless, I'll take the vial to B.R.E.W. and do a thorough scan. Just so you know, I've also used the Vessel to increase the strength of your banishment."

Mezzarix opened his mouth in shock. "What will that do to me?"

She smiled evenly. "It will limit your abilities once more."

He bowed his head solemnly. "I understand. You did what you thought was best."

As Gordy's mom helped Gordy put back on his coat,

Grandpa Rook handed him a small leather book from his shelf.

"What's this?" Gordy asked, carefully handling the delicate pages.

"I keep a journal of my secret creations. It helps clear my head. I scribble down ingredients on even the ones I haven't tested yet."

Gordy looked at him in amazement. "I do, too!" He had never known anyone else other than his mother to share information about a private collection of special potions.

"Of course you do. You're my blood. I want you to take it, Gordy, and study it."

"I can have your journal?"

"Absolutely. After all, since your mother has increased my banishment strength, I don't foresee an immediate opportunity to brew any time soon." Mezzarix brushed Gordy's shoulder with his hand and pursed his lips together. "You know, it may not mean much to you, considering how little we know of each other, but I want you to understand how proud I am to call you my grandson. Maybe one day your mom will let you come back for a visit. What do you say, Wanda?"

Gordy's mom remained straight-faced. "We'll see."

But Gordy knew she had no intention of ever allowing him back to his grandfather's Forbidden Zone.

"Farewell, Wanda." His grandpa looked as though he desired an embrace, but his mom merely nodded. Mezzarix extended his hand to Gordy. "So long, grandson. Take care and be good."

The Stitsers' flight out of Nuuk, Greenland, didn't depart until the following morning, but they had a long journey ahead back to the village several miles south.

"What did you think of Grandpa Rook?" Gordy's mom asked.

Gordy shrugged. His grandfather was nothing like he expected. Gordy couldn't quite think of the right word to describe him, but the word *wicked* probably suited him best. Wicked in a good way. "He's . . . he's not so bad."

She smiled. "And?"

"And he's kind of like me. We can do all the same things. He keeps a potion journal just like I do. It's cool. It's weird, but cool."

Gordy's mom slowed down and came to a stop. She lifted Gordy's chin with her index finger and looked him in the eyes. "He is like you, but the difference is, you're not like him. Do you understand that?"

Gordy thought about it and then shook his head.

"Yes, you both share the same talents. You can do things I could only dream of doing and so can your Grandpa Rook. In fact, I suspect one day you will surpass him in your abilities. You could even become the greatest Elixirist the world has ever known." She pulled Gordy into a hug. "But there is one major difference between you and Grandpa Rook."

"What's that?" Gordy asked, squeezing her tightly.

"You are *good*, Gordy Stitser. And that will make all the difference in the end."

EPILOGUE

Mezzarix sat cross-legged on the floor. Strewn about him were the bones and remains of his dinner. Rotisserie bat had been a little chewier then he had hoped, but his stomach was full and he was content. A light snow had begun to fall and an icy breeze blew in, causing the dwindling flames of the fire to flicker.

Mezzarix glanced up from staring at something in his fingers and startled at the sight of a figure standing in the entryway of the cave. As the figure stepped fully into the room and the soft glow of the firelight glinted off his body, the wizened Scourge immediately relaxed.

"It's been over a month, Doll," Mezzarix said. "I've been lonely."

Doll looked different. He was still all bones and had his same egg-shaped head. But the drawn-on face had worn off completely. Water dripped from his limbs and chunks of ice clung to his ribs. There was soggy seaweed dangling from his chin like a cow's cud, the remaining evidence of

Doll's journey, which had taken him deep into the ocean as he made his way home to Mezzarix's cave.

"What took you so long?" Mezzarix asked. "I've been waiting for your assistance."

Doll made no answer. He stood awaiting his command.

"I need you to gather a few things for me. I know you just got back and are probably exhausted, but I must insist." Mezzarix stood. He still held something pinched between his fingers, but examined a list of ingredients he had jotted down. "Most of these items you'll find on the north end of the property. But you should make haste. A storm appears to be brewing. One that will be quite nasty, I believe." Mezzarix looked at his servant. "What? What is it?"

Doll tilted his head down to one side, pointing to the object in Mezzarix's fingers.

"You want to know what this is?" Mezzarix asked. "This might be nothing." He held out the thin fiber of brown hair. A strand Mezzarix had plucked from his grandson Gordy's head.

"Or," Mezzarix said with a smile, "this might be everything."

ACKNOWLEDGMENTS

Over the years, I've learned just how many people are involved with bringing a story to life. As always, I'd be nowhere without my wife, Heidi. Her support makes everything possible. And thank you to my kids, Jackson, Gavin, and Camberlyn, for acting excited about my ideas, even when they interrupted their normal, everyday thoughts.

I'd like to thank Shannon, my agent, for never giving up on placing this manuscript in the right hands. Your belief in my writing has continually inspired me. Thank you to Chris Schoebinger, Lisa Mangum, Heidi Taylor, and the whole Shadow Mountain crew who turned this book into a force to be reckoned with. And to all those who helped me in the beginning with this novel: Peggy Eddleman, Susan LaDuke, Bryan Bostick, Michael Cole, Jennifer Judd. To anyone else who listened to me go on and on about the story or who read an excerpt or two from this project, you have my gratitude.

Lastly, to my readers: I love you all, and I constantly lose sleep trying to think up new ways to keep you entertained. You're worth it!

GLOSSARY OF POTIONS

A compendium of both approved and unapproved potions, as well as common terms used throughout the potion-making community. Locations listed in italics pinpoint the exact source of where B.R.E.W.'s most-elite Elixirists have worked tirelessly to discover key ingredients to specific potions.

Amber Wick—*Dominican Republic.* One of the tools used in potions to meld ingredients and create a timeframe. Elixirists all over the world use their own variation. Without an Amber Wick, a potion will never fully form because all concoctions require a time restraint.

Anti-Loitering Lotion—*United States of America, Illinois.* A potion that causes the wearer to feel a sudden urge to leave the area or at least not linger in one spot for too long. (Key ingredients: hackberry seeds; cardinal feathers.)

Axiom Application—*United States of America, District of Columbia.* A truth serum that both forces the person to speak the absolute truth and binds them to their promises so that they can't go back on what they've said. (Key ingredient: Jefferson Salamander scales.)

Blind Batching. The ability to concoct viable potions without knowing beforehand the nature or specifics of the ingredients needed or being used. Incredibly rare talent among Elixirists. It is a dangerous practice as the Blind Batcher doesn't necessarily know the outcome of the concoction.

Blogu Goo—*Turkey.* A potion that can make any liquid turn to a solid. Historically used to strengthen mud barriers during times of flooding. (Key ingredient: shaved gypsum.)

Blood Link. A ritual that key members of B.R.E.W. must undergo in order to link their abilities with the Vessel.

Blotched. A Blotched person can be influenced or controlled by an Elixirist. The process is typically done through the application of a potion or through the handling of a Dire Substance.

Boiler's Balm—*Great Britain.* An advanced antibiotic ointment that contains several key ingredients that speed up the healing process. (Key ingredients: loquat fruit; hedgehog molars.)

Booming Balls—*United States of America, Alabama.* Prepared object, generally round and bouncy, that explodes upon impact. Various Booming Balls contain shrapnel and other debris that is launched during the explosion. (Key ingredients: opossum whiskers; honeysuckle stems.)

Canary Bellflower—*United States of America, Utah.* Specially-treated orchid that blooms when the air is clear of toxic chemicals and will wilt when the air is unfit to breathe.

Cipher. One of the most common abilities manifested in Elixirists. Ciphers typically can discern a few key ingredients within a potion and can determine whether or not the mixture is deadly. Gordy is able to Decipher the ingredients in any potion down to the finite details.

Community. Word commonly used to describe those who are part of the Elixirists' world, but more specifically refers to Elixirists residing within the United States of America.

Dampening Draught—*Italy.* Often referred to as an *Inumidire bere* in Italian, this potion will extinguish any form of ignited material, including the most intensely raging fires. It is short-lived though. Once the potion is spent and the flames extinguished, the fire may be reignited. (Key ingredients: tepid Venetian water; dragon's blood sap.)

Decimate Device. Used by Elixirists to destroy a potion or remove a Dire Substance from an object. Not all Elixirists have this ability. Typically falls under the expertise of a Philter.

Detection Powder—*origin varies.* A device used to check potions, ingredients, or other items for Dire Substances, Tainted or Stained items, or traps. Typically comes in the form of a highly-concentrated spray or powder.

Dire Substances. Any ingredient, concoction, or element that has been tainted with the intent to harm.

Disfarcar Gel—*Portugal.* Gel capable of disguising the wearer for a designated period of time. Mostly a few hours, but advanced Elixirists have managed to extend the time period up to twenty-four hours. (Key ingredients: dried Mediterranean chameleon tongue; moldy figs.)

Dragon's Blood—*Socotra archipelago in the Arabian Sea.* Sap from the Cinnabari tree is an uncommon ingredient, but high-level Elixirists generally keep a supply on hand. Most notably used to create Dampening Draughts and other Extinguishing concoctions.

Dram. An Elixirist in training. There are several levels of Dram, from Beginner to Advanced. Gordy is considered a

Dram only because B.R.E.W. has not seen anyone so young with his abilities.

Dual Mixing. A process that requires two or more Elixirists simultaneously adding ingredients to a complex potion.

Elixirist. A term commonly used to describe a potion master. Generally deemed as an elite practitioner of potion making.

Enfetterment Extract—*Egypt.* Binding of an inanimate object to a controlling Elixirist. First used in Ancient Egypt with stone Golems who built the pyramids. (Key ingredients: shattered pieces of a canopic jar; scarab beetle wings; Egyptian beeswax; dried Nile mud.)

Epizootic Egg—*Chile.* Mapuche Shamans use these eggs to capture diseases from the sick and keep them contained. Many plagues have been spread due to the use of Epizootic Eggs. (Key ingredients: Andean condor egg; armadillo skin; tapir eyelashes; poison dart frog venom.)

Eternity Elixir. A self-replicating potion created by Mezzarix that can either enhance the abilities of a particular brew or be used as a substitute ingredient. There are no other potions like it in existence and the potion master who possesses it is virtually invincible.

Goilicanje Juice—*Bosnia.* A potion that causes the inflicted to suffer from the worst case of the tickles. (Key ingredient: visibaba petals.)

Grangou Gruel—*Haiti.* Creates an intense hunger in the inflicted. Believed to be primarily used in voodoo rituals, it has also been the source of some reported zombie outbreaks and bouts of cannibalism. (Key ingredients: bokor dust; solenodon teeth; mahogany seeds.)

Heliudrops—*United States of America, Maine.* Potion that can levitate lightweight objects, depending on the amount applied. (Key ingredient: steeped blueberry leaf tea.)

Kyckling Snor—*Sweden*. Chicken snot is an ingredient commonly used in transfiguration potions.

Miedo—*Spain*. Highly concentrated doses of this fear tonic can cause an individual to fear any object or person identified during the mixing of the potion. (Key ingredients: threads from a matador's cape; Andalusian horse hairs.)

Oighear Ointment—*Ireland*. Instant ice is useful for cooling burns or on hot summer days as a reprieve from the heat. (Key ingredients: shamrock petals; stale, crumbled boxty.)

Pele Punch—*United States of America, Hawaii*. This liquid lava spreads, bubbles, and burns just like lava, but cools instantly when in contact with water. (Key ingredients: angelfish gills; pulverized pohaku.)

Philter. A potion master with the ability to remove ingredients from a potion, thus changing its composition or making it inactive. This is a tedious and difficult job. Most Elixirists display some minor level of Philtering ability, but there are few Expert Philters in the world and even fewer Bio-Philters who have the ability to remove ingredients, potions, and other Dire Substances from a living being.

Purista Powder—*Finland*. Squeezing powder that has varying levels of intensity. Can be used on items to apply pressure, but can also be used to remove objects trapped within tight quarters. (Key ingredients: adder viper venom; brown bear claws.)

Restorator. An Elixirist who can use restorative abilities to replicate any potion through practical means (i.e., ingredients, recipe, etc.). All Elixirists have this ability in varying degrees. This skill also manifests among non-Elixirists at times, though it is mostly dormant in those without the potion making gift.

Risorgimento. A highly illegal practice of using potions to re-animate the dead or otherwise inanimate objects. Typically only dark Elixirists perform such a ritual, but decent Elixirists have been known to use Risorgimento for educational purposes (with permission from the Board, something that is rarely acquired).

Scrute. Process of heating a potion just to the boiling point, dissolving a potion, and applying quicksilver to the mixture. When used in this fashion, quicksilver neither adds nor removes any properties from the potion, but enhances the sensory receptors of a Cipher, which allows them to better identify the ingredients within the potion. This is a risky practice because the Elixirist must know the precise moment to remove the cauldron from the heat in order to properly Scrute and prevent the potion from being destroyed.

Sevite Syrup—*Haiti.* Potion that causes a reanimated object to be in another's control for a period of time. Works incredibly well with organic materials such as soil, trees, or bone. (Key ingredients: tarantula hairs; millipede eyes; lips of a female sea toad.)

Silex et Acier—*France.* Commonly referred to as "Flint and Steel." Two vials of a prepared concoction that is virtually harmless with no effects when used separately, but ignites an explosion of fire when used in conjunction with each other. (Key ingredients: French musket gunpowder; fox fangs; red squirrel saliva.)

Spinnerak Net—*South Africa.* Not as strong as a Vintreet Trap, this potion sprouts a sticky spiderweb-type substance that can trap and incapacitate a target. Some Elixirists enhance their Spinnerak Nets with certain spider venom that temporarily paralyzes their targets. (Key ingredients: baboon spider venom; hissing cockroach antennae.)

Stained. Slang term used to describe the condition of a tainted item, otherwise known as a Dire Substance.

Torpor Tonic—*Great Britain.* Causes a temporary loss of consciousness, approximately ten minutes, but leaves no lasting side effects. (Key ingredients: English Mastiff fur; dogfish shark scales.)

Tranquility Swathe—*British Columbia, Canada.* Potion that creates a web of soft, supple material that, when applied to a target, will make them drift into a deep sleep. The Swathe will also protect the enclosed individual temporarily from most dangerous elements, including extreme heat and cold. (Key ingredients: maple leaf; moose antlers.)

Vessel. The main source of the Elixirists' binding power. It gives them authority to perform Exiles and Banishments, Quench powers, and train young Drams.

Vintreet Trap—*Norway.* Prepared tonic generally contained in a glass vial that, upon impact with desired target, will sprout creeping vines to entangle and constrict the victim. The duration of the potion generally does not exceed forty-five minutes, though that may vary depending on the use of an Amber Wick. The vines weaken over time, thus five- to ten-minute applications are ideal as they can trap the strongest of targets and prevent them from moving. (Key ingredients: musk ox tongue; blue anemone petals; sneezewort seeds.)

Ward. Protective potion used to guard a specific area. It prevents the entry of unauthorized characters and allows for a method for the immediate removal of a person as well. The strength of the ward depends on the rarity of the ingredients used.